MURDER AT CASTLE COVE

Librarian Laurie decides that a literary festival is just what Castle Cove needs, but it becomes clear that not everyone with an interest in the town agrees. As the festival gets underway, so do several sinister occurrences: threatening letters, missing manuscripts — and murder . . . When disreputable crime writer Suzie is sent to the festival, she resolves to blend into the background. But after she bumps into an old adversary and meets a new friend, she is sucked into the centre of a real mystery — one that she is determined to solve.

Books by Charlotte McFall
in the Linford Mystery Library:

HEALING THE HURT
DIFFICULT DECISIONS
RETURN TO RIVER SPRINGS
WISH UPON A STAR
COULD IT BE MURDER?
SECOND CHANCE WITH
THE PLAYBOY

CHARLOTTE McFALL

MURDER AT CASTLE COVE

Complete and Unabridged

LINFORD
Leicester

First published in Great Britain

First Linford Edition
published 2019

Copyright © 2019 by Charlotte McFall

A catalogue record for this book is available
from the British Library.

ISBN 978–1–4448–4336–1

Published by
F. A. Thorpe (Publishing)
Anstey, Leicestershire

Set by Words & Graphics Ltd.
Anstey, Leicestershire
Printed and bound in Great Britain by
T. J. International Ltd., Padstow, Cornwall
This book is printed on acid-free paper

For Tracey

Prologue

Laurie Forster

Laurie Forster sat in the empty library of Castle Cove, the sun blazing in through the windows. She was trying to come up with a plan of how she would be able to keep it open. Hardly anyone came to take out books any more, and the one computer they had seemed to sit idle for most of the week. Except when she decided to use it for checking social media or what books to buy.

Through the window she could see the beach, and watch the tide come in or go out, depending on the time. It was nice watching people playing with their dogs, or on a romantic walk at sunset. Laurie often didn't leave the library until dusk; just because other people didn't use it, didn't mean she didn't.

With no one about, she decided that she would get the drinks ready for the council meeting. Walking into the small kitchenette at the back of the library, she filled a tray with teacups and started the urn for hot water.

Laurie grabbed two bowls, filling them with sugar and little packets of milk. Taking the tray back into the library, she placed it on the table at the far end, behind the biography books. A quiet corner, but it did have armchairs — a place for people to just relax and read the paper, or a book.

Checking the wall clock again, the hands ticked slowly by. She put the 'Closed' sign on the door. How she had once loved working here; now, a grave-yard had more life in it. During the summer, tourists used to come from miles around to Castle Cove, yet no one came to the library. Not many people came here now, either; they preferred the delights of Cornwall's larger seaside towns. Laurie felt that there was a fine line between attracting tourists and ruining the peace and tranquillity of a small town.

She heard tires screeching on the

tarmac outside the small building, signalling that the council members had started to arrive. Laurie rushed back into the kitchenette, bringing out the hot-water urn. Why wasn't she surprised to see who the first person was?

'Mr. Arnley, I'm so pleased to see you.'

Grunting, he shook her hand, and proceeded to pour himself a drink.

She had the distinct impression that only she cared for the library, such was her passion for books — especially the Queen of Crime, Agatha Christie. Those were stories she could read over and over again. That was when it had hit her — a way to get more tourists and people into the library.

Castle Cove was a quaint little seaside town. The winding cliff-side road gave wonderful views of the sea and beach below, and the library stood on the high street, squashed between the post office and the Castle Arms, a pub-cum-B&B. It wasn't a tourist trap like the bigger seaside places on the same stretch, but was a great place to come and relax. Laurie had grown up here, so knew it well.

When everyone had turned up for the meeting, Laurie shuffled her papers, making sure that everything was in order. 'I have been thinking that we need to get more people here, into the town.'

'Go on.' Mr. Arnley raised his eyebrows.

Really, is it that distasteful? she thought. 'I wondered about organising a Literary and Murder Mystery Festival.'

That got a lot of urns and ahs, but no real comments.

'Look, I think it is best for the town . . .'

'Who would you get to come?' Mrs. Ainsworth asked in her high-pitched voice.

'Obviously we need to advertise in local writing magazines. Contact publishers and so forth.'

'Mr. Arnley, you're not seriously considering allowing this?'

Mr. Arnley's face grew a horrid puce colour. 'We need to do something, Mrs. Ainsworth.' He handed the blank pieces of paper around. 'Right, we will vote.'

'Why is that? That new hotel and golf

course over by Castle Point would bring in the tourists.' Mrs. Ainsworth sniffed indignantly.

'I'm sorry, but a lot of people wouldn't want to see a massive hotel complex here. We need to vote.'

The conversation was at an end. The twelve members of the town council hid their pieces of paper out of sight from everyone as they placed their votes.

Laurie collected them and totalled them up. 'The votes have been counted, and the winner — by eleven votes to one — is having the festival.'

'I hope you realise, Ms. Forster, that you will fall flat on your face.'

'Thank you for your vote of confidence.'

Anger bubbled up inside Laurie. Mrs. Ainsworth was one of those people who loved the idea of a golf course and hotel. As long as it was an exclusive place to go; *none of the riff-raff*, she'd heard her say. She felt much relief that her plan seemed to be working; now all she had to do was get others to agree to host events. The sailing club? Perhaps even the school would be happy to lend them the hall? The whole thing could end with a murder mystery night and a meal at the Castle Arms. She had been to several similar events herself, and knew just how much fun they could be. It didn't take a genius to realise that Mrs. Ainsworth was the one who voted against the plan.

When the meeting was over, she cleared away the tea things and headed straight out to the pub. Hopefully Des, the landlord, would be quite happy to have all seven of his B&B rooms full for the entire week. It would take a while to organise. Maybe she could get it done for the beginning of September ... She needed the season to still be in full swing; that way, she would be able to get summer visitors.

⋆   ⋆   ⋆

Some weeks later, it was all finalised. Her festival would start on a Friday night, and continue until Thursday. Laurie was looking forward to it, and to all the talks from some of her favourite authors. If the reporters loved it as much as she did, then next year's event would be even bigger. Everyone had said yes to hosting part of the event, and Des had been more than happy.

1

Suzie Cail

Thirty-two-year-old mystery writer Suzie Cail's eyes were heavy with dark shadows. The lack of sleep had caused her insomnia to get much worse. Her once glossy auburn hair was now lank and dull, after events of the past several months had caused so many problems. The dark office she now sat in, with its heavy old-fashioned furniture, darkened her mood.

Sitting in an oversized leather armchair across from her agent, she felt dejected and hurt. The case had gone against her. Seriously, all she had done was admire a plot she had been discussing with another writer, and go on to write her own version. How wrong could she have been? The judge had found that it contained too many similarities to the other author's work. Even though Suzie's own novel had come out first.

She remembered how she had felt when her laptop had been stolen at the very beginning of her career. Its contents soon appeared on the shelves as a bestseller, and that computer was the only proof she had that she owned the story. Unfortunately, she wouldn't get it back — nor the Wedding Shop Mystery novel that was the first in a three-part series based in Yorkshire.

Suzie had an idea that an ex-writer friend of hers had taken much too much of an interest in her novel, asking all sorts of questions. Then, this friend's own book — based in a flower shop — came out, taking Suzie's idea. This wasn't illegal, but the words she had used were all Suzie's own. Melissa Spencer had a lot to answer for, and Suzie would make sure that she paid for what she had done.

Well, you lived and learned. Her career as a mystery novelist was in tatters; she had been all over social media, in the papers, and even the radio stations.

The silence in the room was deafening. Why wouldn't, or couldn't, they just say she was finished, and get it over and done with?

Her agent, a grey-haired man, sat with his long fingers stroking his beard, his weasel-like eyes staring down at her. 'I'm sorry, Suzie, but right now, we both believe that you should take a sabbatical from writing and from London. After all, for the time being no one will want to purchase your books, and there are too many negative things being said about you right now.'

'But I didn't do anything wrong!' Suzie guessed she could say anything she wanted, but no one would listen to her. Her heart sank into the dark depths of her stomach.

'The court says otherwise, and that is what we have to do,' he said, shuffling papers on his desk. 'There's a festival you have been invited to attend. I would advise you to go.'

'You want me to what?'

'I will not repeat myself. I am sure you heard me the first time.'

'So, this festival you want me to go to?' Suzie needed to change the subject, and hoped that they would forgive her for whatever they thought she had done wrong.

'Well, the lady running it is a Ms. Laurie Forster. It's a totally new inception. So I couldn't tell you how many people will be there or not.'

Her agent clasped his hands together, twirling his thumbs; he always did this when he was thinking hard about things. Straightening her skirt as much as she could, Suzie sat dumbstruck. Great; now they were pushing her to the back of beyond. In the hope of what? That she would disappear and never return?

'It's in Castle Cove, a little seaside town — although I would call it a village.'

His voice grated on her nerves. 'So when do I go to this hidey-hole?'

'The festival starts on Friday, and lasts until Thursday evening. I suggest you go home and pack. Get someone to take care of the kids and cat or whatever.'

Suzie was desperate to find out who had wanted her place at the top of the murder mystery tree. For five years she had held onto that position — albeit by the skin of her teeth, but she had — and now it was gone. 'I didn't do anything! How many times . . .'

'Well, unfortunately Suzie, the judge and now the public,' he replied, holding out the day's paper, ' . . . all disbelieve you.'

'I don't have a cat or kids.' Her agent was probably too busy to even bother realizing that, or did he actually care?

Great. If even her agent didn't believe her, what hope did she have to salvage her reputation? 'Fine, whatever. Can I go now?'

'Of course. Our relationship is on hold, at least for the time being.'

Suzie stood quickly, grabbing her bag, storming out of the office and slamming the door behind her. She had to go home and pack for a stupid half-hearted mystery festival, in the dark depths of the English seaside. If only she could have proof that Melissa Spencer had stolen her ideas and words, then she would be in the clear.

After the hour she'd had, it felt good to get into the safety of her London flat and head straight for her pale pink bedroom. Nothing was out of place: she was very particular about the way her things had to be. Even her socks had their own drawers depending on the colour and type of material they were made out of.

Taking a small bag from the bottom of the wardrobe, she started packing enough stuff for the trip as well as her precious laptop. A half-finished manuscript that she might be able to complete; but she was stuck, and the words didn't flow like they used to do. For a writer there was nothing worse than staring at a blank page for hours and days on end.

After searching the internet for accommodation, she found the Castle Arms. It was a suitable base; Suzie gave them a quick call and sorted out a room. What other choice did she have? Now all she had to do was get down there and speak to this Ms. Forester and glean as much detail as she could.

Picking up the phone again, Suzie called her best friend. 'Hey Jess, I wondered if you wanted to come around?' She drew silly patterns on a piece of paper whilst she waited for her answer. 'Great. I'll see you soon.'

She wandered between her en-suite bathroom and her bedroom, putting things neatly in her case. At least Jess believed her. Her friend was a romantic novelist for one of the top six publishers; a newbie to the field of writing, and yet one who had had her dream fulfilled quicker than some.

The doorbell rang. Suzie ran down the stairs to answer it. 'Jess!' she shouted, hugging her friend on the doorstep.

'Are you going to let me in, or are you going to leave me standing here?' Jess smiled.

'Come in. I'm just packing.' Standing aside to allow Jess to enter, then closing the door behind her, she headed back upstairs.

'Suzie, what on earth is going on? Why are you packing?'

She took several calming breaths before she answered. 'Well, according to my publisher and beloved agent, I need to go away for a week to some stupid seaside town.'

Jess sat on her bed, twirling her hair around her fingers — honestly, that was so annoying, Suzie thought. 'Well, after that court case, people don't want my stuff or me around.'

'Nice.' Jess pulled a face, which Suzie took to mean she wasn't impressed either, but couldn't do anything about it.

'So I have to show my face at some idiotic literary festival. I'm not sure that it will do any good.'

'I don't know, love; just go with the flow.' Jess picked up the heart-shaped pillow of the bed, hugging it.

Yes, that was just how Suzie felt at the moment. 'Anyway, I have to go, but it's a three-hour drive from here. I don't suppose . . . ?'

Jess shook her head viciously. 'I have deadlines to meet and that party on Thursday.'

'Remember me while you're having fun.'

Suzie had been thinking for a long time about getting out of the Smoke. London was way too hectic, and she often got herself lost on the blasted Underground.

Traffic here was gridlocked most of the time, so even though she had a car, it wasn't conducive to use it unless she was leaving the city. Perhaps she would see a nice town or village on the way down that she could move to . . .

'I can't stay and chat long.' Jess threw the cushion on the floor, and Suzie flinched, wondering why it couldn't have been put nicely away.

After finishing packing her bag, she zipped it up, placing it near the door. On double-checking the state of her bedroom, nothing was out of place — apart from the cushion. Her red laptop case balanced precariously on her bag — *don't fall*, she chanted in her mind.

'Listen, Suzie, just do what they say for now. You might even come up with an awesome bestseller down there.'

'Nah, I can't even put words on the page at the moment.'

Placing the cushion back in the centre of the bed, grasping for her things, she followed Jess out of the bedroom. After checking that she hadn't left any appliances on, and that the windows were shut, she lifted the keys off the hook in the hallway. 'Bye, Jess. I'll see you in a week.'

★   ★   ★

The drive down to Castle Cove was long and arduous, all those twisty twining country roads making her feel sick. The sky was blue and clear; not a cloud hung in it. Suzie knew that what she was doing, although initially it had seemed wrong, was in fact the right course of action. Even if her blood still boiled at the thought of her career in utter ruins: ashes to ashes.

It was around three o'clock when she arrived on the edge of the village. Several quaint cottages lined the road. Her lips tingled with the salty air, and from out of the window she could just see the beach and smell the fresh scent of the sea. It would be a good idea to bottle that smell; there must be something in it, because it always made you hungry. Fresh-caught fish and chips eaten as you sat on the promenade, she thought; there

17

wasn't anything better.

Checking the map that lay on the passenger seat, she realised that she actually was, for once, going in the right direction. Even though her journey was going well she couldn't get over the feeling that she had been dumped high and dry in the back of beyond. Just because her publishers would be happy to get rid of her. Bringing her hands forcefully down onto the steering wheel, tears stung the backs of her eyes as she desperately tried to regain some equilibrium. No one would want to come to see her, and no one would come to this stupid festival.

She didn't want to admit to herself that in actuality the so-called plagiarism wouldn't have happened if she could have thought up her own book. Yet each time she sat down to write, for hours the blank screen would taunt her.

This Laurie woman had sounded like a real cow on the phone, making out it was her that was having to repay her debt to society, her fans, and most of all to herself. She had let everyone down badly.

For now, there was no way out, except to go to her fate.

2

Laurie Forster

'Laurie, have you sorted out the accommodation yet?'

'Of course, I have, Mr. Arnley,' she answered, keeping her voice edged with attitude. Who the hell did he think he was? *It's that council of cronies that will be the end to everything I hold dear*, she thought. They hadn't even helped her sort it all out, for goodness' sake; they didn't care, as long as that new damn hotel went up. To hell with the literary festival and the whole of Castle Cove with it.

Her blood boiled. She felt the heat and anger rise up like a phoenix from the ashes. *One day, Mr. Arnley, the rest of the community will know what you are really up to. Even if I have to go to the national press.*

Slamming the phone down onto the cradle, she got up from her desk, walking purposefully into the kitchen. Coffee, that was what she needed: strong, black, and thick enough to stand a spoon up in.

Looking at the wall clock, she saw it was nearly time to go over to the pub and greet those authors that were arriving tonight. All the information packs and the murder mystery night things lay scattered on her desk. A black cloud of apprehension hovered overhead — if this all went wrong, she could lose her job, and even her home.

Laurie had decided that all the people that came and took part in the murder mystery evening as part of the literary festival would take on the roles of the characters. All the other ones she had been to had only had actors who'd taken the parts, whilst the guests would just try and figure out who did it and why. They had always been fun — except for the last one she'd attended, where one group had made it hard for anyone else to hear.

She picked up all the murder mystery packs, then her bag and jacket. Now ready, she went off to the pub.

The car park was packed with vehicles, and for some reason Laurie was becoming nervous. The worst thing that could happen was that the literary festival failed miserably.

All the tables in the Castle Arms had been moved to the sides of the main room of the pub, and rows of chairs filled the floor. Pictures of the local countryside decorated the walls, and a pool table was hidden behind an archway. On a shelf above the bar were two dozen Toby Jugs in a variety of styles. It looked like your typical country pub, with a board full of specials emphasising the use of local produce.

They had placed a whiteboard at the front, just off to one side; it was to be used to add the odd clue to the crime. This was where she would stand. It was a daunting task. She didn't want anyone ruining her master plan to save Castle Cove from the hotel that would ruin the life the residents had now.

Whose bright idea was this, Laurie? Oh, yes — yours!

People began filling the room, and she

recognised several authors and publishers. The famous crime writer Martha Holt. Aileen Keyes, one of her favourite historical authors. Mr. David Robinson, who wrote cosy crime — she had read all of his series.

She was dressed down in jeans and trainers — much better when she was sat down or working in the library. Her mother had once said that women of her age didn't wear jeans. Honestly, some people! Jeans were for everyone regardless. They were comfy and versatile garments. Besides, she was forty-five, not two. Laurie had to laugh. *Mothers! Who'd have 'em?*

Laurie stood to one side, waiting for everyone to be seated before she began her welcoming speech, and taking several calming breaths before moving to the front of the expectant audience.

'Welcome, ladies and gentlemen, to the first of hopefully many literary festivals in Castle Cove. There will be talks by Aileen Keyes and Martha Holt, and several other renowned authors. Throughout the weekend there will be a murder mystery event!

I have your packs here, and all those taking part will receive a character sheet and backstory. The person who is the killer needs to please keep that quiet!'

She received a few moans of *Yes, we know*. Well, it was probably a little obvious; but during the events she had previously attended there was always one clever so-and-so who interrupted the whole piece and shouted loudly who the killer was before people had finished the first course.

'I hope you all have a great week; if you need anything, just ask. I will be around for the whole event.'

$$\star \quad \star \quad \star$$

Suzie sat hiding at the very back of the seating arrangements. Taking part in a murder mystery week wasn't the way to keep her head down in the author community. She was still kicking herself for going to that writing conference, and listening to Melissa Spencer and her idea for a romance book. Suzie had only heard a few lines of the idea, called an 'elevator pitch', but she had loved it. Then she'd created her own version of the idea — all totally legal! But for some reason Melissa had won the court case, despite having released her book six months after Suzie's had come out.

Suzie wondered if the judge had been bought off. Melissa had told her she was no good at writing, and that Suzie's was better than her own, which had nearly made her give up. Finding an original plot idea was like plaiting fog, after all. But that was then, this was now.

The speech was being lost on her. Suzie's head was full of woe, and the dark cloud hanging over her refused to go away. But perhaps here, in the midst of all the other authors and publishers, she might regain her love of writing.

Sat next to her was a blonde-haired girl who was busy taking notes and looking extremely scared. Suzie wondered if this stranger recognised some of the authors there, for when they looked at her she looked back down at her notebook.

'Hi, I'm Suzie Cail.'

The girl looked startled to have been

spoken to so directly. 'Crystal Siena.'

'Is this the first time you have been to a literary festival?' Suzie asked.

'Yes. I don't generally do well meeting new people.'

Suzie could understand that. She had been like that once, preferring to stand by the wall and watch the world go by. Crystal would soon come out of her shell. *She* had, eventually. Though she had yet to meet Aileen Keyes personally, they had conversed by email and over social media. She was such a nice woman to talk to.

'Suzie, are you taking part in the murder mystery thing?'

'I'm not sure; I wasn't planning on it. My agent and publisher told me to come, and all I was going to do was hide away and enjoy the fresh air. What about you?'

'I think it could be fun. All I have to do this weekend is go over my manuscript and hope that it's fine for my publishers. I'm just so worried that it won't be right.' Crystal replied.

'Yes, I know that feeling. You go from elated one minute to thinking that your latest story is utter rubbish.' *Yes, Suzie, you know that feeling all too well*, she thought to herself.

'Look, I know we've only just met, but . . . would you take a look at my manuscript for me, please?'

What a cheek! I've only just met her, and she's asking something like that!

Oh, come on, Suzie, you used to be the same. What harm can it do to look?

'Sure, I'll read it tonight.'

'Thanks. I'm so unsure of the story.'

'Crystal, you're just too close to it now. I know the feeling when you can't see the wood for the trees. That is why you can't see if there is anything wrong with it. I promise that it gets better, honestly, but that feeling of your manuscript being rubbish never really goes away.' Suzie wanted to make Crystal feel good about herself, but she had a feeling she was only making things worse.

'You know, I'm sure I read that you had been in court!'

'Yes, well, there's no defence when your laptop is stolen and someone else publishes your story.' Suzie folded her arms, trying to protect herself from the line of questioning. Would she have to answer this all week?

'I didn't mean anything by it. I didn't think you had done anything wrong, anyway.'

'What?'

'Look, Suzie. How she got away with it, I will never know.'

Crystal's brows knitted together, and Suzie was grateful for the vote of confidence. 'Thanks; you're one of about two.'

'I think there are many people who believe you.' Crystal patted her hand.

Suzie had a feeling that this new author would be someone she could talk to. 'I'm not going to the suspense talk. How about we meet back here later for a drink and something to eat?'

'Sure. I'm staying at Michaels' Hotel. There was no room at the inn, so to speak.'

Suzie laughed for the first time in a long while. She looked at her watch and then at the timetable, which she had managed to extract from the envelope. 'How about in two hours?'

'Yes, I think each talk is only an hour. The one after is on plotting. I'll have a look at that one, too — hopefully it will be interesting.'

Suzie had no intention of partaking in anything to do with the festival. Just because she had been made to come to this godforsaken place, didn't mean she had to mingle. Besides, she hated to mix: large crowds scared her. Talking to one or two people was all right, though. It wasn't a good trait in an author, to not like mingling — that was what her agent said.

Suzie said goodbye to Crystal. Pushing her chair back, she prepared to leave the Castle Arms. A walk along the cliff top would be just the thing. As she walked past the rows of chairs, she had a feeling that everyone was watching her. What were they saying? Were they discussing the court case? A shiver ran down her spine. As she reached the door, Crystal handed her the manuscript, and Suzie thrust it into her bag. It was then that she saw Melissa Spencer sidling into the room.

Suzie didn't have a Dictaphone, but

she was sure one of the shops in Weymouth carried them. Something discreet, so she could catch her telling the truth about everything . . . The idea crashed around her brain. Yes, she would do it. And then Melissa would pay for everything.

Laurie, the woman Suzie assumed was in charge, cleared her throat, interrupting her reverie. 'Those who would like to take part in the murder mystery event will need to come and get a pack from me. The idea is that each participant takes a role, and for the week you will be that character. The investigation — *The Curse of the Ankh*! You need to discover who stole an ancient Egyptian Ankh, decorated with hieroglyphics and rubies; what the motive was, and why museum curator Lucas Roberts was murdered.'

Suzie looked down at her pack, fiddling with the sheets of paper and trying to find the timetable.

'The first talk — being held in a few minutes over at the library — is on romantic suspense. Tomorrow all the talks will be held at Michaels' Hotel, just along the cliffs towards the old lighthouse. You can't miss it. I will finish my speech now, and thank you again for coming.'

★ ★ ★

Laurie handed out all her murder mystery packs. It was great that so many people wanted to take part. She hadn't been sure when the idea had struck her — just that it might be a good plan, a way to rescue her one true love: the library.

Mr. Arnley approached her, wearing a grey and white checked suit. 'Looks like the literary festival is only a minor success. There aren't as many people here as I expected.'

'What do you mean? All the hotels are fully booked. The restaurants will soon be packed.' Was this guy totally crazy? People had to stay in Weymouth itself if they wanted to come. She had purposefully done both day and weekend tickets to account for different people's budgets — and tastes. She had been to several festivals to see how they worked, but not all the talks were enjoyable — some were downright boring.

Laurie looked past Mr. Arnley and saw the now-infamous mystery writer Susie Cail sat talking to someone she didn't know — just a person who enjoyed a murder mystery night, she assumed. 'Mr. Arnley, if you have nothing of value to add, I must ask you to excuse me.' Walking away from him, she was struck by the sight of Suzie taking a manuscript from the unknown person.

She had some out-of-favour writers here, and that included Suzie Cail. Though she couldn't remember what she had done. But would her presence here put the cat amongst the pigeons? Only time would tell. Oh, well — it was none of her business as long she didn't cause trouble for her. Laurie didn't need any trouble, least of all from Mr. Arnley, but she could be almost sure that he was going to cause trouble for her.

When Laurie finally walked out of the Castle Arms the sun had gone down, the waves crashing against the rocks in a crescendo. Laurie loved nothing more than sitting on the cliff edge watching the sea, but tonight she was more stressed than she'd thought she would be. Perhaps she would go and sit there now, relax for a while — that was, unless someone joined her and rudely interrupted her.

There was nothing that she could do except see how the week went. *Hey-ho, that's something for another day*, she thought to herself.

★ ★ ★

Suzie walked along the cliff edge, breathing in the sea air and tasting the sea salt on her lips. She was thirty-two, and her career was already over before it had really begun. Melissa was a bit younger than her and was always, whenever she saw her, dolled up to the nines in full makeup and high-heeled boots of the sort that witches wore in films. She was surprised at how tranquil this place actually was. Earlier today, she'd been ready to disappear. Anywhere else, even Mars, would have been preferable to here. Everyone watching her. Were they talking about her behind her back? That Melissa

Spencer would happily say anything to anyone that would listen. For weeks, she'd had magazines and journalists phoning and knocking on her door.

The peace here was surprisingly pleasant. Perhaps, when she got back to London, she would try and find somewhere like this.

Suzie sat on a bench near an old lighthouse. The actual town seemed so tiny in the distance; she hadn't realised just how far she'd walked in such a short space of time. She took Crystal's manuscript out of her bag and started to read it by the streetlight. Not that this was ideal by any means, but the sooner she had the manuscript back in the rightful owner's hands, the better. Hopefully she would have read it before Crystal had finished the two hours of talks.

Suzie doubted that she would get a story out of this week — not that anyone would want to buy anything she had written.

3

Crystal Siena

Crystal wandered over to the library. She had been looking forward to the festival since her publisher had mentioned it. The town was buzzing; so many people were walking in the same direction as she was. She wondered how big the library was, and if it could fit so many people inside.

Standing across the road was a man with a baseball cap over his eyes. Crystal wondered what he could possibly be doing, just hanging around when everyone else hurried here and there. She shrugged her shoulders and decided that it was not really any of her business.

Everyone she had met so far had been really nice, especially Suzie. These writing courses were a great thing to do; you always picked up hints and tips from other authors. Even story ideas, sometimes — but, as Suzie had found out, that led to trouble.

If she was totally honest with herself, she had done the festival as a way to get out of Sheffield for a while — away from her ex, who continued to hound her even though they had broken up six months previously. Crystal had the sudden idea of inviting Suzie to come up and visit sometime; she seemed like the kind of friend she needed.

Finally, she arrived at the library after taking a wrong turn and going in totally the opposite direction. The queue was snaking out of the door, and people jostled to get in. She waited patiently for her turn to go in; once she did, she saw the whole place was packed.

Tracy Quilford stood beside a whiteboard; a wooden table and chair beside her. 'I think everyone that is coming is here, so I will start. Welcome to 'Writing Romantic Suspense'. I have written eleven novels so far; all but a few are romantic suspense, and I've had all those published in large print as well. Most of the novels have been published by *People's Friend* and as 'My Weekly' Pocket Novels'.

Crystal was impressed; she had read the pocket novels, and the quality of the writing was second to none. Taking out her notepad and pen, she began making untidy notes on everything Tracy said.

'You don't need a lot of romance in them, as the murder and the solving of the crime should be at the forefront . . . '

Tracy continued in this vein for an hour, and Crystal was a little miffed when the talk was finished. She could have gone on to listen to a lot more of what she had to say. Perhaps they would have a chance to chat during the next week? She had gleaned quite a few ideas, and a plot was forming in her head . . .

Crystal headed back to the Castle Arms where the next talk was being held. There were a few people here for the plot talk, though not as many as there had been a few minutes ago. She wanted to learn as much of the business as she could, and find out where she was going wrong — if indeed she was. There was a dinner on

Tuesday for everyone, and that was something else she was looking forward to.

Crystal sat next to an auburn-haired woman dressed in a very severe-looking black trouser suit. The woman turned to her. 'I'm Melissa.'

'Crystal. So, what sort of books do you write?'

'Romance, although I am doing my Master's degree in crime fiction.' She spoke with a strong but put-on voice in a northern accent.

'Sounds interesting,' Crystal replied, not really interested.

'I have a few author friends doing it as well.'

The superior snob, Crystal thought.

'Do you have a book out?' Melissa enquired.

'I will have; my first novel is out next year.'

'You know, I have one out now, and four more being published by a big romance publisher.'

Crystal had a feeling that Melissa had to be the best writer she knew. Why would she boast about her publishing contracts if not to rub people's noses in what she had and what they didn't? There was always that one snob who liked to gloat that they were better than you. When Crystal had first started, she had met someone like that, and it was because of them that she had nearly given up writing altogether.

She was glad that she hadn't listened to them . . . but had another new and nervous writer listened to Melissa Spencer? Crystal's inspiration for becoming a writer was so very much like Suzie's own. The more she thought about it, the more Crystal realised that Melissa wasn't a nice person.

The plot talk dragged on, and it was only in the last fifteen minutes that anything decent was said: 'Don't go too fast,' a major problem that she herself had. Looking at the Mickey Mouse on her watch, she saw that it was nearly time to go back to the Castle Arms and meet Suzie.

Finally, the author thanked them for coming, and then came the obligatory applause. Crystal grabbed her bag, hurried out of the library and went back to the pub. When she got there the wooden tables and chairs had been put back into the right places. Her shoes stuck on the floor from all the spilled drinks, the landlord wore a small leather waistcoat and a t-shirt that looked much too small for him. He seemed like a middle-aged biker; the sort you see hanging around the seafront or café's. He had a kindly sort of face and greying hair.

The open fire had been lit and a lovely warmth emanated from it. Crystal could imagine sitting in front of it, toasting marshmallows on little sticks and drinking hot chocolate. Suzie hadn't arrived yet, so Crystal ordered a drink and took a seat next to the fire. What was it about country pubs and open fires, which had most people making a beeline for them?

The door to the pub opened and Crystal could see Suzie walking through with what looked like her manuscript in her hand.

'Crystal, did you enjoy the talks?'

'Yes, although I was commandeered by

some author who did nothing but talk about herself.'

'You do find some people are like that.' Suzie paused before handing back the manuscript. 'I really enjoyed it — the last chapter has a few too many head-hopping paragraphs, but other than that . . . '

'Thanks, Suzie. I mean, I know I don't know you very well, but — '

'You know, I think you will be the richest twenty-six-year-old around when that comes out,' Suzie replied, patting Crystal's hand.

Crystal smiled shyly. 'I'm being rude; would you like a drink?'

'Just a tea, please. I don't drink,' Suzie replied.

'You don't drink?' Crystal laughed.

'Why is that so funny?'

'I just hadn't met an author before that doesn't love a tipple every now and again.' Crystal smiled. 'I'd best get those drinks.'

Crystal got up and went over to the bar, and Suzie sat looking around. The place was virtually empty, at least for the time being. The Toby Jugs had caught her attention when she had walked in earlier: they looked funny. Perhaps she would buy one or two when she got home, if they sold any down Portobello Market.

Crystal came back with the drinks. Over her shoulder, Suzie caught sight of Melissa Spencer coming in. For a moment they looked at each other for longer than was appropriate. Suzie broke the eye contact and looked into the fire. The last thing she needed was to have a conversation with that snake.

'Hey, Suzie. Are you okay? You look like you've seen a ghost.'

'I'm fine; just saw someone I want to avoid, that's all.'

They sat in silence for quite a while, until Crystal decided to break the ice. 'Suzie, I know you are worried about Melissa, but she isn't worth the hassle.'

She tried to smile, but it came out all wrong. 'I know, but that ultra-superiority thing she has grates on my nerves.' Taking a sip of tea, Suzie glanced around the pub: it was starting to get busy. Several of the guests had notebooks and pens in hand and were asking questions of each guest. They must be the murder mystery lot; she hadn't even looked at the pack Laurie had given her.

'What has she done?'

'Oh, she just thinks she is better than everyone else. Take her house, for example: she lets you believe that she owns her home, but in reality she rents it. I know renting isn't a bad thing — but it's her lies, you know?'

Crystal nodded.

Suzie looked like she wanted to change the subject. 'Where are you staying?'

'Over at Michaels'. I'm actually going to head off there now,' Crystal said, getting up out of her chair. 'Will I see you tomorrow?'

'Yes, sure. I think I will have a wander around Castle Cove for a while.'

Crystal wondered what Suzie could possibly be doing, just hanging around for hours, when there was so much going on that would be fun for her. 'Goodnight.'

Crystal left the Castle Arms, turning left. It was so quiet outside. Stars twinkled brightly in the sky, and a bright moon cast its light onto the sea.

A dark figure stepped out in front of her. 'Hello, Crystal.'

Crystal gasped. 'Mathew, what do you want?'

'Oh, some of that advance would be nice. I need money.'

She tried to walk away, but he grabbed her arm. 'I said, I need money.'

'You won't get anything from me. Now just leave me alone.' She broke free and ran as fast as she could to the hotel. Her heart was beating so fast, it was as though it was going to break out of her chest.

Crystal got to the safety of the hotel; opening the glass doors, she walked towards the reception. It was empty, so Crystal rang the little bell on the counter and waited, all the while looking over her shoulder at the door. What was Mathew doing here? He always needed money; he gambled everything he ever got his hands on.

Crystal was extremely worried. Her new publishers had plastered her six-figure advance all over social media. She had tried to tell them not to: she'd known only too well what Mathew would do if he knew how much she — or, rather, her manuscript — was worth. She was going to be a fairly wealthy woman, especially if the Bridge Murders series did as well as she thought it would.

'Hello, can I help you?' asked the receptionist. He was a nice-looking man with a red tie and blue suit. If only she was in the market for a new beau, Crystal would have picked him.

'I have a room booked for the week? Crystal Siena.'

'Yes, Ms. Siena. I'm Colin; if there is anything you need, please don't hesitate to contact me.'

Colin gave her a key with a large number on the keyring. 'You're on the fourth floor — just go up in the lift and turn right, and your room is the last one on the corridor.'

'Thank you, Colin,' she replied, taking the key and heading off to the lift.

Crystal arrived at her room, and was pleased that she had a sea view and an en suite bathroom. She wondered what sort of room Suzie had over at the Castle Arms.

She could be really happy living here. She had decided that she was more interested in the talks than the murder mystery. Of course, she had done them before, but she never got the murderer!

Crystal unpacked her bag and flicked the kettle on. She hunted around in her handbag for her notebook and pen, making a note of Mathew's arrival in Castle Cove and what he'd asked her for. The police had told her to keep a diary of his threats that they could use in court.

She sighed and put the notebook away. When the kettle had boiled she made herself a cup of tea. Once it had been made, Crystal got ready for bed — she had a lot to think about. Was it the right thing to have charges brought against her ex? He hadn't done anything except ring constantly and accost her in the street.

Grabbing her cup of tea, Crystal got into bed and settled down for the night.

4

Laurie Forster

Laurie congratulated herself on a job well done. Des had told her that the Castle Arms was fully booked, as was Michaels' Hotel. Mr. Arnley hadn't seemed particularly happy that things, at least on the surface, appeared to be going well.

Her phone vibrated on the kitchen table. She picked it up, and a message flashed on the screen: *You won't save the town.* She didn't recognise the number, so she wrote it down. Maybe she would try calling it tomorrow.

The doorbell rang; Laurie got up, checking the kitchen clock. Nine-thirty in the evening was rather late for anyone to be making a social call.

Cautiously, she peered through the little peephole. Standing on her doorstep was Mrs. Ainsworth. 'Yes?'

'Can we talk?' Mrs. Ainsworth shouted

through the door.

Reluctantly, Laurie opened her front door. 'Didn't we say enough to each other at the meeting?'

'I know we don't always see eye to eye, Laurie. But you need to listen to me or else things will happen around here.'

Laurie wondered if she was a sandwich short of a picnic. 'I'm sorry, but I don't think that I understand you correctly.'

'Look, this literary festival of yours was a great idea, but there are people on the council who want it to fail.' Mrs. Ainsworth invited herself to sit down.

'Hang on — you voted against me?' Laurie snapped.

'No, I didn't; I voted *for* the literary festival. You honestly think, girl, that I want a great big golf course and hotel ruining things for the businesses of this town?'

'What?'

'I know what I said at the meeting.' Mrs. Ainsworth's voice became more high-pitched. 'I had only one option — I've had threatening letters telling me to vote against your idea and allow the hotel.'

Laurie walked over to the kettle and flicked it on. 'How about a cup of tea, and we start again?'

'That would be great.'

'So, how about you go back to the beginning?'

Mrs. Ainsworth sighed. 'Colin Michaels is my grandson, and if the new hotel was built, he would be out of a job.'

'I honestly had no idea that Colin was your grandson.'

'We don't speak about it much. Mr. Arnley would say that I was giving Michaels' Hotel preferential treatment. What you have to realise is that some on the council want to see the destruction of the town. If we had a golf course, Castle Cove as we know it would not exist — people would leave, and the land would be worth a fortune for others who want to change everything.'

Laurie was shocked — but was Mrs. Ainsworth telling her the truth? 'Why would someone want all the townspeople to move out?'

'The land on which Michaels' Hotel stands, for example, is worth half a million pounds. The house prices around here would go through the roof. If no one comes, then the prices go down. You know how it is.'

Laurie held up a cup. 'Tea?'

'That would be lovely.'

Laurie prepared the tea. Her mind was whirling as questions assaulted her. Who on the town council didn't want the town to survive? Too many questions, not enough answers. After everything Mrs. Ainsworth had said in all their other conversations, she'd seemed as though she didn't like her.

'Penny for them?' Mrs. Ainsworth said.

'Nothing, just thinking that we haven't always got on.' It was more a statement of fact than a question.

'I'm sorry, dear, but someone threatened to cause trouble for me in regard to several old votes I had made.'

'What sort of votes?'

'I stopped the Carters doing a basement conversion, as it would have meant digging underground. My house could have been affected, you know, with all the drilling. I'm sure that you know how these things go. That could have shifted the foundations of my home — then what would I have done? I am only surprised you didn't know about that.'

'How many people in this town talk to the wacky librarian?' No one really did talk to her, even though she was on the town council. Laurie knew her head was so full of books that even if people did speak to her, she probably wouldn't pay that much attention.

'Probably more than you think,' Mrs. Ainsworth replied, her voice soothing. 'I'd better go. Just be careful, Laurie. I have a horrid feeling that something is going on.'

The two of them got up, and Laurie saw Mrs. Ainsworth to the door. After her guest had left, she locked and bolted it. The hairs on the back of her neck stood up on end. She wanted to laugh; after giving her conference attendees a murder mystery, she had her own mystery to solve!

★   ★   ★

Suzie settled into her room at the Castle Arms, having already made a cup of tea. She sat up in bed looking at the murder mystery file, reading and re-reading it. She figured out who had done it and why. Not a very difficult one to solve, but she wouldn't ruin it for the people who wanted to play. Picking up her phone, she called Jess.

'Hey. No, I'm bored.'

'So why don't you try and write?'

'I can't think of anything, and who would buy it anyway?' Suzie twisted the sheet between her fingers.

'Look, Suzie, you need to stop all this. You need to get back on the horse, so to speak.'

'I guess.' Suzie listened to Jess prattle on for another few minutes. Jess could talk about nothing for hours, and she wasn't really in the mood. She had only made the call because she was bored, and also to check in, letting Jess know she had arrived safely.

'Are you going to let someone ruin your career?'

'What can I do?'

'Putting pen to paper would be a good idea,' Jess retorted.

Suzie cut the call short soon after that, and snuggled down to sleep.

Sunlight peeked through the gaps in the curtains. Suzie pulled the duvet over her head. It was too early. What would she do today, whilst everyone was sitting listening to talks? Go for another walk? Find a tall, dark and handsome stranger? Or try and do what Jess had suggested and write?

Suzie managed to drop back off. When she woke again, the clock on her bedside said it was eleven. She had slept too late for breakfast, and she had no idea where Crystal was. Did she care? For some reason, she did; talking to Crystal was better than walking about here by herself.

Suzie jumped in the shower, then dragged her stuff out of the suitcase she had brought. Normally she would have hung everything up, but this time she hadn't even bothered.

Opening her door, Suzie stopped in her tracks. There was shouting, but she couldn't be a hundred percent sure what was being said. She stayed on the landing, edging closer to the top of the stairs. A dark-haired guy was shouting at Des; he seemed to be asking where Crystal was staying. Des wasn't allowing him upstairs to check all the bedrooms.

Suzie had no idea who he was, but she didn't think she wanted to meet someone like that. When he had gone, she walked downstairs, to be met with Des.

'Are you alright?' she asked.

'Yes; takes more than that to bother me.' Although Suzie wasn't too convinced by what he had to say. 'You're missing all the fun over at the literary festival.'

'To be honest, Des, I'm not bothered.'

'Look, lass, you need to put the past behind you. Let them talk; people are always happy to pull you down. Just ignore them,' he said as he cleaned the tables.

'You know who I am?'

'Of course! Laurie over at the library was saying who she had got coming. Besides the fact that I have read your books.'

'Thanks — I think.'

'You know, it's about time you had a new one out. What is it you write again — murder mysteries?'

'I did, but after the court case . . . well, I've stopped writing.' Suzie picked up a couple of the glasses on the table and moved them onto the bar.

'Look, if you're fed up of wandering around here, you could help out behind the bar if you'd like? I can pay you with meals, cash, or free room and board — whatever you want!'

'I'd be happy to do it for some of that shepherd's pie you have on the menu for later!' Suzie smiled at him.

'Done deal,' Des replied.

He always seemed to wear a leather waistcoat and jeans. Des wasn't the typical landlord — but then, what did the typical landlord look like?

'Suzie, if you come behind the bar, I will show you how to pour a decent pint.'

'I'm not going to put people off, am I?'

Des threw the cloth onto the bar. 'Why do you think that?'

'I was once told by Melissa Spencer

that I had absolutely no talent for writing, and to give up.'

'Now that *is* rude; you have had several books published. How many has she had — just the one?'

'I think she has. One that came out six months after my own.'

'Yes, I saw all that in the *Castle Cove Gazette*. It was a big story. So, do you want to tell me your version?'

'I thought you were showing me how to pour a pint, Des.'

'Aye, I was.' They walked behind the bar, a row of optics behind them all freshly filled. 'So, grab a glass from underneath the bar. I don't need to tell you that you want a pint or a half-pint . . . '

Suzie grabbed a pint glass and waited for further instructions. It took several attempts to pull a decent pint without a large foamy top.

'You'll do, lass,' declared Des. 'So, are you going to tell me?'

'About three months before the release of *Bridge Murders*, my house was broken into. All that they stole was my laptop. Even knew where I kept it when it wasn't sat on the desk.'

'So you think someone you know did it?'

'Yes, but I can't prove my theory.'

'You think this Melissa stole it, or had it stolen?'

Suzie grabbed a bar towel and began to wipe down the bar, 'Yes. There is no other reason that she would then produce a book which came out, and she had her own version. She did an eBook first, and then a paperback, as some of the publishers do'

'Was there anything else on that laptop?'

'Just some old poetry. I generally only kept one manuscript on my computer at once. Otherwise I get too confused as to what I am supposed to be working on — a novel about a wedding shop, or one about a murder!'

She looked at him now, and it was as though she could see the cogs of his brain turning. 'Des, what did that guy want?'

'He wanted to know if some lass called Crystal was staying here.'

'No.' *Thank goodness*, Suzie thought

to herself. 'She's staying at Michaels' Hotel. I should really warn her.'

Suzie took out her mobile and phoned Michaels'. She needed to let Crystal know. Whoever this bloke was, he seemed dangerous, at least to her.

'Could you please get a message to Crystal Siena, and tell her some guy called Mathew is trying to get to her?'

Suzie ended the call and put the phone back in her pocket. She hoped that Crystal would be okay. At least she would see her tomorrow. Apparently there was to be a meal at the Castle Arms as well as the murder mystery thing.

She was kept busy until closing time at eleven that night. After helping Des put the glasses in the dishwasher and clean all the tables down, Suzie yawned; this pub work could be tiring. 'Want me to help out tomorrow?' she asked.

'Aye, lass. Homemade chilli for dinner. I got some chef from Michaels' to do the meal for tomorrow night's shindig. Couldn't be bothered mesen; too much like hard work, and I do enough of that already.'

Suzie laughed. Des was a character; he always seemed to have something to grumble about. She could get used to being around him, and Castle Cove had something about it she liked. What if she was to stay, and never go back to her poky house in London? Who would care that she wasn't there? Jess, true — but she had her own life, and things had been strained since the court case anyway. Maybe she would have a look in the estate agent's and see what was available.

Suzie slept well that night for the first time in months; the fresh sea air and working at the pub must have helped. Next morning she got up, washed, dressed, and went downstairs, hoping that she would be able to work at the pub on a full-time basis if she could find a house here.

It was a huge surprise to her that she wanted to even move here, but the beautiful coastline was a draw — and the people were okay too. Laurie, the woman who ran the library, seemed a bit too strange for her tastes, though.

Des was sat at the bar, a cup in one

hand, the other flicking through the pages of a newspaper.

'Morning,' Suzie said cheerfully.

'Morning, lass.'

'Des, I was . . . I was . . . ' *Just ask him! The worst he can say is no.* 'Do you need any full-time help?'

'Yes, it's just me and I don't get much time to do things I need to do.' He looked at her, confusion etched on his face. 'Planning on staying?'

'I'm thinking about it. Castle Cove is a really nice place, and I need a fresh start. Maybe I will do what you suggested and write another novel.'

'And I want a signed copy,' Des said with a grin.

Suzie nodded. 'So, what do you think about a new barmaid?'

'Of course, you're hired. That means I will have to actually pay you, and not just in grub.'

'Well, that is a cross you will have to bear.'

'Go sit down, love, and I'll bring your food.' Des pointed over to the tables. Suzie did as she was asked and waited patiently for her full English. Des had a way of knowing what the customers wanted before they had even asked.

Her phone vibrated. Taking it out of her pocket, Suzie looked at the text message. *On my way over to the pub — Crystal.*

After about fifteen minutes of her waiting and playing a silly game on her phone, Des brought over her breakfast.

'Thanks, Des. My friend Crystal is coming over. Would you let her in, please?'

'Of course, love. Anything for you.'

As she was eating, a knock on the pub door alerted her to Crystal's arrival. Des unlocked the door and let Crystal in before locking it again. Now wearing a red gypsy top and black skirt, Crystal looked like a Spanish senorita.

'Hey, sorry, just finishing my breakfast.'

'It's okay. I'll wait.' Crystal sat down opposite her. 'Thanks for the text, but Mathew had already accosted me when I left here.'

'Who is he?' Suzie asked, eating the last piece of toast.

'My ex. He has a bad gambling addiction. Hence he is my ex — it's a shame that he couldn't kick the habit.'

Suzie caught the wistful look on her face. 'So, if he *had* kicked the habit . . . ?'

'I would have taken him back. But I can't see him ever doing that.' Crystal shrugged her shoulders. 'Are you going to any of the talks today?'

'Yes, I might do. But I did say I would help Des later. There's the dinner tonight — I don't know if I'm taking part, or working for my supper.'

Des must have heard her as he shouted over, 'No, enjoy yourself, lass. I'll have enough help tonight.'

'Fancy being my date then, Crystal?'

'I'd love to. Look, come to the talk about character creation and plot arcs; it will be fun, and I'm sure it will help you get back on track.'

'Okay, sure, but it won't get me back on track. I can't leave you all on your own,' Suzie replied.

Suzie finished her breakfast. Picking up her plate, she took it into the kitchen and washed it. Drying her hands on the tea towel, she headed back out into the bar. Des and Crystal were talking, and didn't notice her at first. As soon as they did, they stopped chatting. Suzie had an awful sinking feeling that they were discussing her. Why else would they have stopped speaking?

5

Suzie Cail

'You ready? I washed up, Des.'

'Thanks lass, I'll see you later.'

Suzie followed Crystal out of the pub. They walked down the main high street and turned up towards Michaels' Hotel. Suzie loved the way Crystal dressed, uninhibited by the latest fashions in all the glossy magazines. If only she could be so brave herself.

Most of the talks were being held at the hotel, and those that were undersubscribed were held at the library. The literary festival was a waste of time in Suzie's eyes.

'Suzie, are you ever going to write again? I loved your Detective Inspector Holland.'

'I'm sorry, Crystal, but he's finished.'

Suzie thought she could detect a hint of disappointment in the way her new friend spoke. She did miss her detective — he had been around for a while, and she had already thought up a new crime for him to solve. She would have set it in the Norfolk Broads, but Castle Cove was a great alternative location.

'Don't let someone like her let get you down. Seriously, I'm sure if your publisher saw a great novel from you, then they would snap your hand off.'

Suzie pulled a face. This new friend of hers wasn't going to let up anytime soon. 'Can we drop it, please?'

'Whatever,' said Crystal.

They arrived at Michaels' just as it seemed every other attendee did too. Suzie would be able to hide at the back with no one saying anything to her. Crystal could go and sit elsewhere if she wished, but the back was safe.

The talk started with mention of a rainbow plot arc. She had heard of them, but never really thought of them like this before. The sessions lasted until three, and by that time Suzie had had enough. 'Crystal, I'm going back to the pub to help Des.'

'Okay. See you at the dinner.'

When Suzie arrived back at the Castle Arms, Des was putting the finishing touches to the decorations. It looked like a Halloween theme with all the skeletons and spiders' webs. Black and purple covers had been placed on the tables and chairs. At one end a stage had been set up, and a large pumpkin nestled in between a cut-out of a haunted house and a ghost.

It did look really good, and Suzie felt bad for not helping after Des had been so kind to her. 'Des, this looks great.'

'Thanks, lass. How about you earn your meal and blow up some balloons?'

'Oh, if I have to,' she said, smiling at him.

She had forgotten how hard it was to blow up balloons. Hadn't they invented an easier way of inflating them instead of using all your puff? He only wanted twelve, and as she was blowing up the final black balloon, Suzie felt utterly grateful that it was the last one.

'I've finished now, Des — want me to help hang them up?' she asked.

'No, you go and get yourself sorted. It starts at six.'

Suzie nodded and headed upstairs. She would get her glad rags on and try to enjoy the murder mystery night. Looking at her watch, she realised that she was tired. A nap, that was what she needed, even if it was only for an hour; the black cloud which hung over her head was making her tired.

She opened the door to her room, grateful for a bit of peace and quiet. She lay down on the bed and closed her eyes, letting sleep take her.

A loud noise outside her window woke her up with a start. Normally she would be grumpy that someone had dared to disturb her. Today was different; if she wasn't there for the start of the murder mystery night, Crystal would be disappointed. The one thing that would put a dampener on her evening was if Melissa Spencer was going.

Suzie jumped in the shower, dried herself off, and grabbed a pair of black trousers and a purple blouse. She had no idea what she'd packed when she left

London, but this outfit seemed to go with the Halloween theme that was going on.

Reluctantly, she headed downstairs. She could hear a lot of noise; it looked like the night was getting started already. Suzie took a deep breath, descending the stairs slowly; she was hoping that Crystal was already there or, at worst, that Des needed her behind the bar.

Melissa was stood at the base of the stairs, looking at her. 'Oh look, it's Miss Plagiarist,' she said nastily.

'Melissa, go away. We both know what you did.'

'Do we?'

Suzie realised pretty quickly that Melissa wasn't going anywhere. 'Yes. Now, if you will excuse me, I need to find someone.'

'I have another contract for a new book. About an injured soldier, if you want to know.'

'Not really. I'm not interested.'

Suzie pushed past her. An injured soldier! Another idea she had had at one point, and shared with Melissa. How could the two of them ever have been friends, when everything in the friendship was all about Melissa, who cared only about herself?

Suzie pushed the conversation out of her mind and looked around trying to find Crystal.

Lots of people had already picked seats. Crystal was sat at one of the side tables out of the way. They would have a good view of the stage for when the performance happened. After not even wanting to join in at first, she was now hoping that she could win the little contest they held, and beat Melissa.

'Hey, Crystal.'

'Hi — what did she want?' Suzie was shocked, and it must have told on her face. 'I saw Melissa accost you as you came down the stairs. I'm sorry I didn't rescue you; if I had, we could have lost the table.'

'No worries. She wanted to tell me about her new book — about a soldier — and that she knows what she did. Except for the fact that she won't admit it in court so at least my reputation would come back.'

'You should just ignore her. That woman isn't worth your time or energy,' Crystal stated. 'Do you want a drink?'

'I'll get them; what do you want?'

'A J.D. and coke, please.'

Suzie went over to the bar and jostled with the others that had lined up two people deep. Part of her wanted to jump the queue, or just go around the back of the bar and serve herself. Des and a girl with a blue mohican were serving. Suzie shouted over the noise of the crowd, 'Need a hand, Des?'

'Nah, lass, but you can blooming well serve yourself!'

That was all the invitation she needed. Suzie walked round the back and helped herself to a J.D. and coke plus an orange juice, placing the money in the till. This wasn't going to be a great night, she could tell — for one, it seemed really noisy, and there were so many people. Where had they all come from? It was surprising that Des could fit everyone in the pub!

Suzie looked over at Crystal; her friend looked as bored as she was. Taking their drinks she went to sit back down. There were several people wearing various outfits, from witches to Dracula and Frankenstein. Suzie wanted to laugh at them, but she assumed that they were part of the murder mystery night cast.

Dracula appeared on stage, and the voices faded away to nothing, 'Welcome to our Murder Mystery Night — you can join in and try to guess the murderer at the end. There will be prizes for the winner. We will be sat with some of you during dinner, please ask us any questions you wish.'

Crystal nudged her. 'Are we having a go?'

'Sure, why not?' Suzie was happy to have a friend.

The actors and actresses started their little play as several waiters came around laying prawn cocktails in front of each patron. How on earth did they know what people wanted? She certainly hadn't been asked, but then again she was a rush job.

A lad with messy hair approached their table, 'I need money, Crystal. I know you just got a large advance.'

'No! Mathew, I'm not giving you any. Stop gambling, and you would have some cash,' Crystal snapped back.

'Look, you have no idea how much trouble I'm in.'

'So what do you want me to do about it? If you borrow money from people you shouldn't, then it's your own fault.'

'Crystal, please. I love you. I need help — I'm begging you.'

'No. Mathew, I'm sick and tired of your antics. You're just making a fool out of yourself — and for goodness' sake, lower your voice.'

Suzie looked around. Everyone was staring at their table. Just then she saw the girl with the blue mohican approach them.

'Hey, you need to leave now. Before I throw you out,' she said. With that, she grasped Mathew's arm and dragged him towards the door.

Suzie couldn't help but smile. That girl had guts; she'd buy her a drink later. 'Crystal, are you okay? Who is he?'

'My ex, I told you.'

Suzie felt bad for forgetting that

Mathew was her ex. He did seem really desperate, not vicious at all — just a very troubled young man. Maybe if she spoke to him then he would leave Crystal alone. He needed help, and to go to one of those support groups — but would that get the people who were after him off his back?

★ ★ ★

The murder mystery night was now in full swing after a starter of prawn cocktail and a main of chicken breast and vegetables. They were just waiting for whatever dessert was coming their way. Frankenstein had been murdered, and everything was pointing to Dracula — except that Suzie didn't trust the witch. She discussed her theory in hushed tones with Crystal, and they both agreed they would go with her.

The time came for them to fill out the sheet and the reason they had picked that particular murderer. 'Are we still going with that?' Suzie asked, looking at Crystal, and suddenly noticing Melissa was walking past them. She covered her sheet over so that their writing wasn't seen.

'Yes, let's. I did like her; she was pretty funny.'

Suzie wrote everything down, even going onto the back of the sheet, as there wasn't enough room for their reasoning on the front.

One of the murder mystery cast came around and took their sheet as a waitress brought over sticky toffee pudding and custard. Suzie was reminded of being a schoolgirl and eating it at dinner.

'Would you do a literary festival again?' she asked Crystal.

'Yes, I think I would, Suzie. I've had fun with all the talks, and some people have been nice. What about you?'

'I've actually considered staying — selling my flat in London and buying somewhere here.'

'Really?'

Suzie picked up her virtually empty glass and took a last sip of orange. 'Yes; the sea seems to agree with me. I've been thinking of a new murder mystery — *Death in the Highlands*.'

'I'm glad you're getting back on the horse, so to speak. What's it about?'

Crystal looked really interested in what she had to say. 'To be honest, I'm not sure. I need to get properly started . . . but I've got a magazine editor in my head as the killer.'

'I'd love to read it when you have thought things through a bit more.'

'Sure, Crystal — happy to let you read it.'

Suzie wasn't sure what all the magazine editors would think of one of them — even fictional — being a murderer. It would actually be fun to find out.

Dracula approached the stage with the troupe of murder mystery actors, and gave a small speech thanking them. He had a few pieces of paper in his hand, and the witch had quite a few in hers.

'I just want to thank you all for taking part. We had so much fun, and so many questions. Anyway, we had quite a lot of wrong answers.'

The witch held up her pile of papers, and then Dracula continued his little spiel. 'There were three right answers.

One group gave a lot of information about the whys and wherefores, and so they are the winners.'

He held up a sheet; instead of the back being plain white, it was covered in writing. Suzie nudged Crystal and nodded towards the paper.

'The winners are Suzie and Crystal! Could you come up here and claim your prizes, please?'

They stood up and walked over to the stage. Suzie couldn't help but feel smug — she had beaten Melissa at her own game!

'Here you go, girls — well done!'

Dracula handed them each an edition of the complete Sherlock Holmes stories. Suzie loved the detective; once she sat down and flicked through the pages, she realised the writing in the book was so small she would need a magnifier to read it. They had a certificate each too, which simply said 'Super Sleuth'.

Suzie couldn't help but glance over at Melissa, who had her arms folded across her chest and looked like she had swallowed a wasp. Suzie couldn't help but smile and silently gloat.

'Hey, do you want another drink?' she asked Crystal, eyeing the bar, which was really quiet.

'No, thanks. I'm a bit tired; think I'm gonna head off soon.'

'I'll see you tomorrow? Apparently, this murder mystery is a preview for the main one then.'

'Yes, course. Anyway, I'm off — night! I've had a good evening.' Crystal picked up her certificate and book and headed off out.

The pub was still full of people chatting, drinking, and generally being loud. Suzie would give Des a hand to get the pub back into shape, but first she would put her book and certificate upstairs out of the way. 'Des, I'll be back!' she shouted above the noise, but getting no answer from Des, she assumed he hadn't heard her. His blue-mohican barmaid was off collecting glasses again. She looked young, as though she had only just left school.

Suzie ran up the stairs two at a time. Unlocking her door, she put everything on the bed before heading back downstairs. Walking behind the bar, she started to take out the clean glasses, putting them back on the shelves under the bar top. With the dishwasher now empty, she reloaded it with all the empties which were scattered around on the bar top.

People eventually made their way out of the pub, Suzie glad that the noisy crowd were off to their respective hotels and homes. Was this what a busy night at the pub looked like? Des looked like he was dead on his feet: he certainly needed help.

'Des, you look shattered. Why don't I lock up and tidy up for you?'

'That'd be grand, love, you and Jamie could do it between you.'

Suzie had actually been wondering what the blue-haired girl was called. Des walked out of the swinging door, leaving the two of them alone.

'Anything you want me to do first?' she asked Jamie.

'You could start by collecting all the glasses. We'll put the tables back when that's been done. Oh, you'll find another dishwasher in the main kitchen.'

Suzie did as she was asked. With the two of them it didn't take long. She hadn't seen Melissa much after their confrontation at the base of the stairs. But she seemed to be getting very chummy with Aileen Kaye. She wondered what they had been talking about. With any luck, she hadn't discussed any of her ideas — Melissa would only steal them. She would lure people into a false sense of security with her friendship, and then steal their stories.

'Can you give me a hand, please?' Jamie asked.

'Yes, sure. So, how long have you been working here, Jamie?'

'Since I left university.'

Suzie was surprised. Jamie was certainly older than she'd originally thought. Looking at her, she was the sort of person you would consider crossing the road to avoid. She wore black Doctor Martens, a black top, and skinny jeans. A typical goth if ever she saw one.

'You looked shocked!' It was a statement of fact, rather than a question.

'I am, a bit. You look a lot younger.'

'Yes, I get it all the time. To be honest, it is quite annoying.'

Suzie laughed loudly. Oh, to be young again!

When they'd done, they said goodnight and Suzie, tired but happy, wrote *Death in the Highlands* in a notebook. Maybe her publisher would be interested. Suzie had decided, somewhere between putting the glasses away and clearing the tables, that she would write the story.

6

Suzie Cail

When Jamie had gone Suzie looked around the quiet pub and wondered what she would do now. Sleep wasn't going to come easily tonight. Des had given her a key to get in and out. Maybe a walk along the front again would make her sleepy. One thing she hadn't expected was to hate the festival but love the area. Suzie wanted to do some more exploring and find that perfect seaside hideaway.

Suzie tried going upstairs as quietly as she could; she wanted to change into her jumper and then go for a little walk. The step next to the top creaked as she stood on it. 'Stupid stairs,' she muttered.

She grabbed her coat and headed off back downstairs, being careful to avoid that step. The street outside the Castle Arms was quiet; you could have heard a pin drop. Suzie didn't bother looking both ways as she crossed the road. Suddenly, headlights were bearing down on her and a car screeched to a halt mere inches away from her.

Turning to face the motorist, her heart thumped in her chest. *That was close*, she thought to herself. Taking a deep breath, she walked to the driver's window and knocked on it.

The black privacy glass did nothing to tell her who was inside; she could be making a huge mistake. You never knew what a driver could be like. Suzie knocked again. The window came down. Sat inside was a rather good-looking man, ruggedly handsome rather than model-handsome.

'You should watch what you're doing. You nearly ran me down,' she said icily.

'Don't you think you need to look?' He shook his head, then put his arm out of the window. 'How about we start again? I'm Ryan Arnley.'

Suzie hesitated and then took his hand. 'Suzie Cail.'

'As an apology, do you want to go for a drink sometime?'

'I'm only meant to be here for the

festival, and it finishes in a couple of days.'

'How about tomorrow? Will you let me take you over to Taylor's Restaurant? The best fish and chips in the county.'

Suzie let out a little laugh. 'Who says they are the best?'

'Me.'

Suzie laughed again. 'Well, I'm staying at the Castle Arms. If you wanted to know.'

He nodded. 'I have to get back, I'll see you tomorrow, Suzie Cail.'

'Bye,' Suzie replied, and instead of going for her walk, she walked back to the pub. A stiff drink or a nice cup of sweet tea would do the trick. How could she have managed to get a date after almost being run over? You couldn't credit it.

She'd watched him drive off in a very expensive car. Well, he might never even bother coming back. She wouldn't be surprised if he went home and Googled her, and decided he would be safer staying away.

★   ★   ★

Suzie was awoken by the sound of sirens blaring loudly. It sounded like they were right outside the pub. She got up and drew the curtains back. Below her window there were several police cars, seemingly in a line. Something had gone on. And she'd thought it was such a quiet town.

Dressing quickly and without much care, Suzie rushed downstairs and outside. Police officers were standing around, with several more near the cliff edge. 'What is going on?' she asked a rather burly policeman.

'I wouldn't look, miss, a young woman has died.'

Suzie didn't know what to say. She had never been faced with a situation like that before. Taking out her mobile, she tried ringing Crystal, but her phone went straight to voicemail.

Maybe she was still in bed — after all, it was just after seven in the morning. Suzie walked away from the scene; no doubt it would be the talk of the town. She sent Crystal a text: *Crystal, phone me when you get up.*

Suzie walked back to the pub. Opening the door, she found Des standing there, nursing a cup. 'Hey, Des, you okay?'

'Yes, just not totally with it first thing in the morning, and I would have preferred it if I hadn't been woken by a load of noise.'

'Apparently someone's died. Not sure where or why, the cops wouldn't tell me.'

'We will find out. Why don't you have a drink? Thanks for your all your help last night.'

'It's alright, glad to help.'

'So, have you thought any more about moving here?'

'Yes, I did think about going down to the estate agent's today to see if there was anything available.'

Des looked thoughtful for a few minutes, and then flicked through the pages of his local paper. 'There's a cottage for sale in the square. Apparently it's a fixer-upper; obviously means it needs major work doing.'

'I'll have a look; it's on the way to Michaels' isn't it?' She asked, a little confused as she hadn't been to the square yet.

'Yes. Instead of turning left on the way to the hotel, turn right and you're at the entrance to the ginnel. Go through the ginnel and it's right there,' Des said whilst he scribbled directions on a beer mat.

'Thanks. Can you tell Crystal I've gone to have a look at the house, please?'

'Of course. I'm not sure if she will come in,' he said.

Suzie was serious about moving down here. It was so quiet and nice. She'd phone the estate agents and get them to come and value the house. She was just going to leave the pub, when a knock on the door startled them both.

'Answer the door, lass.'

A horrid feeling came over Suzie, and her stomach churned. She unlocked the door. Standing before her were two police officers.

'Yes?'

'Can I speak to the landlord, please?'

'Des, there's two officers to see you.'

'Come in.'

Suzie stepped aside and let them in,

standing rooted to the spot, the door still open.

'Can I ask your name, sir?'

'Yes, it's Des Moxin.'

'We were wondering if you knew a woman by the name of — ' The policeman paused whilst looking in his notebook. ' — Crystal Siena.'

'No . . . hang on. Isn't that your friend, Suzie?'

'What . . . what's happened?'

'I think you'd best sit down.'

'No. No, I won't sit down. Every time someone tells you to sit down, it's bad news.' Suzie was shocked — the police and ambulance must all be there because of Crystal.

'Crystal was found dead this morning by a walker.'

'What happened to her?'

The officers exchanged glances. 'We believe she was murdered.'

Suzie hadn't realised that she'd walked to the nearest table until she sat down. It was all so surreal. Crystal was only here last night, and now she was gone . . .

A glass was suddenly sat down before

her. 'Drink,' she heard someone say, as she looked at the shot glass like it had materialised out of thin air.

'We need to ask you a few questions. When was the last time you saw Ms. Siena?'

'Last night, after we won the murder mystery thing. She said — she said she was going back to the hotel.'

'Did you arrange to meet today?'

'Yes; I tried phoning and texting her, but she didn't answer,' Suzie answered in a rather monotonous voice.

'Have you any idea why she was in Castle Cove?'

'She was here, like all the rest, for the literary festival.'

The police officer that had been asking all the questions put his notebook away. 'What's your name?'

'Suzie Cail.'

They shared a look between them and turned back to face her. 'We've heard of you. Found yourself in trouble with the police before, haven't you?'

'That's if you believe that thief — then, yes.'

'You're staying at the hotel, I presume.'

'No, here.'

'We may need you to answer more questions at another time. Please don't leave town.'

'Don't leave town' — *that's what they say in those silly detective programmes on television*, she thought to herself. Suzie was in shock, wondering what had happened to Crystal.

The officers left and Suzie found herself ushered away by Des. 'Go have a lie-down.'

He stopped short of actually taking her upstairs; how she got up the stairs on her own, she had no idea whatsoever. Suzie unlocked her door, and curled on the bed like a cat. Part of her didn't want to close her eyes, but she wanted to shut out the entire world.

Suzie must have dropped off, as she was awoken sometime later by a loud banging on her door. 'Hang on,' she said sleepily.

Rubbing her eyes and straightening her top, she walked sleepily to the door. Two burly police officers were standing on the landing. 'Ms. Suzie Cail?'

'Yes.'

'You're under arrest for the murder of Crystal Siena. Could you come with us, please?'

7

The tallest one, with blond hair, said to his partner, 'Search the room.'

Suzie was just grateful that she wasn't being led out of the Castle Arms in handcuffs. Scalding hot tears ran down her face. This was unreal. It had to be a dream: she would wake up in a few minutes, lying on the bed.

Des was nowhere to be seen as she was frogmarched out of the pub. A small crowd had gathered and several people took pictures. Wonderful: now she would be all over the papers tomorrow — again!

The officer opened the patrol car door, bent her head and pushed her inside, slamming the car door behind her. Her heart sank as flashes came through the glass. She didn't see any point in hiding her face. She knew she was innocent. It was just another bad week in the world of Suzie Cail.

She sat quietly in the back of the police

car, contemplating how she had even found herself in this mess. It seemed to take an age to get to the police station, but it couldn't have been more than a few minutes. The roads were quiet; the only sound in the car was the buzz of the radios.

They arrived at the police station, and she was processed into the system and placed into a cell. Grey concrete walls, and a small bench with a blue mattress, were for now her only friends. It was all so ridiculous and yet it was all too real.

Suzie tried going over all that had happened since last night: she had helped Jamie tidy up, gone for a walk, returned, locked the door, and gone to bed. That was it — nothing more, nothing less.

Crystal had left the pub, feeling tired. After that, Suzie had no idea of what she'd done. Then, this morning, she had tried to phone and text Crystal, but had got no reply. Would the police check her phone? Of course they would.

The door to the cell swung open.

'What?' Suzie looked with disdain at the female officer.

'Can you come with me?'

Suzie padded in her socks to the interview room, where a small tape recorder sat on a table. Two chairs were placed either side of the desk; and one, for some reason, against the back wall. Suzie was wondering where the lamp was. The Spanish Inquisition came to mind.

'Ms. Cail, this interview is being recorded. We found this in your room during our search.' The officer pushed Crystal's manuscript towards her.

'What? You can't have found that in my room. I gave it back to Crystal.'

'So how did we find it in your drawer?'

'It was put in there. How can you think that I would kill my friend or steal her manuscript?'

The officer looked at her, but was stopped from saying anything else by a tap on the door. Another officer peered around the door, 'Can I have a word?'

Tutting, the officer got up, leaving the room for a few minutes. Suzie couldn't hear what they were talking about. It seemed an age before they came back into the room, and both just looked at her.

Neither seemed overly happy.

'Interview terminated at twelve-oh-eight pm.'

'Ms. Cail, come with me.' She was led out back to the custody suite and over to the desk rather than to the cells.

'You're free to go for now. Don't leave town; we may need to speak to you again.'

Suzie couldn't believe they were just letting her go — no charges, no nothing. Part of her wanted to ask why she was being released; the other part of her thought she was better off just getting out.

Suzie grabbed her stuff from the custody sergeant, who showed her out of the police station, slamming the door behind her. She was in complete shock. Something must have happened for them to have basically kicked her out of the station. Especially when they had been so sure that when they arrested her, they had got their woman.

She had no idea why she was still gazing at the now-closed door. She should get away from here as soon as possible. Go back to the pub, because she certainly didn't want to go back in there.

'Excuse me, Ms. Cail, do you need a lift back to the hotel?'

The male voice made her jump, turning quickly around. *Great, another copper — just what I need.*

'Thanks, but . . . '

'No, get in. I'll give you a lift. Least I can do.'

Suzie looked for a way out, but she was at the other end of the town — nearer to Weymouth than to Castle Cove. 'I guess. You're not going to arrest me again?'

'No, should never have arrested you in the first place,' he said. 'I'm Bill, by the way.'

'I don't need to tell you my name. So, have you any idea what was going on?'

'It's normal to question the last person to see the victim. We go by the last person to have seen them usually being the killer,' Bill said, matter-of-factly.

'Look, can you tell me what happened to her?'

'Looks like she was hit on the head and pushed over the cliff. They did find her manuscript in your room. The boss said all the pages had been moved around, as though it had been read.'

Suzie looked at Bill and then stared out of the window. When she had given the manuscript back to Crystal, she had made sure that the pages were all in the right order. Maybe Crystal had messed them all up when she had gone through it — perhaps she had found something wrong?

'Have you no idea at all?'

'No, but I would stay out of Detective Inspector Tay's way.'

'Who killed Crystal? She was such a sweet person.' Although Suzie wasn't expecting him to answer. And why was he warning her? Did he think she was going to look into her friend's murder? Too damn right she was — whoever had hurt Crystal should spend a long time behind bars.

The little cottages flashed past, and it wasn't long before she was sitting in the car outside the Castle Arms. Suzie breathed a sigh of relief; her freedom could be short-lived. If the inspector decided to re-arrest her, there would be nothing she could do.

'Thanks for the lift,' Suzie said as she climbed out of the car.

'Here's my card, for if you remember anything. Or need anything.'

He smiled at her. Suzie waited until he was out of the way before she went inside the pub.

Camera flashes went off as people surrounded her. 'Ms. Cail! Did you kill that author?'

'Have you got the stolen manuscript?'

'Over here, Ms. Cail!'

Reporters and crews flashed cameras and shoved microphones in her face, bombarding her with questions. She tried to push past them all. She wouldn't cry. They must have been waiting outside the police station, seen her leave, and followed her. Perhaps there were already some hanging around her home, waiting, biding their time until they caught up with her.

A flashy car pulled up alongside her — just in time, too. Ryan got out of the car, wearing tight-fitting jeans, a black shirt, and black boots. He looked very hot; Suzie attempted to put her eyes back in her head.

'You been causing trouble?' he asked.

'Just get me away from these vultures.'

Ryan had to see she was surrounded by the press, Suzie was beginning to feel trapped; she saw no way out. If he didn't do something, she was going to scream very loudly.

'Ms. Cail won't be answering any questions.' Ryan steered her away from the gang of press.

'You may as well know, seeing as the whole town will by now. Especially with them around.' She nodded towards the press that were still standing on the opposite pavement, talking into microphones or Dictaphones. 'An author has been found dead, and I was arrested for her murder.' She tried to hold back the tears.

'Did you do it?'

'No, I didn't. She was my friend.' Suzie turned away and walked into the pub.

She didn't care that she had left Ryan standing on the pavement. After all, he was just someone she'd met the night before.

In the pub, the noise was unbearable. Someone must have noticed her, because all of sudden it went deathly quiet.

Suzie tried her best to keep her head held high as she walked through the crowds and upstairs to her room. The police hadn't asked her before the interview if she wanted a solicitor, so perhaps that was the reason she'd been let go.

★　★　★

Ryan stood open-mouthed, looking at the closed door. He had only met Suzie last night, but was sure she wasn't capable of killing someone. She was pretty in a strange way . . . not model-good-looking, but there was just something about her.

His dad wouldn't approve — in fact, he never approved of anything. Mr. Arnley Senior was only interested in the stupid hotel and golf course that would, if planning permission was given, destroy the town. Ryan had, in his own way, tried to stop his dad from going ahead. He wouldn't listen; he never did, just always did what he thought was best.

He turned to get back in the car. Maybe later he would come and see Suzie? *No*, he thought, *I'm going to talk to her now*. Slamming the car door shut, he went into the pub.

He shouted over to the bar, 'Des, alright if I go up and see Suzie?'

'Aye, lad. She's in the first room near top o' stairs.'

Ryan flung open the door, climbing the stairs two at a time. The door was closed, and a *Do Not Disturb* sign was hanging on the knob. He knocked anyway. Suzie was upset and he wasn't going to allow her to be alone.

'Go away!'

'Suzie, it's Ryan. Open up.'

'I don't want to see anyone.'

Ryan knocked again and then said, 'I'm not going anywhere. I can stay here all night if I have to!'

The door clicked, opening a small bit. So all he could see of her was her eye. 'Ryan, I'm in no mood for any visitors.'

'Look, let me in. I get the feeling you could do with someone to talk to.'

Suzie opened the door slowly. Ryan spied a chair sitting under the window, and once she had opened it sufficiently, he made a beeline for that. Suzie stood by the door, her hair messy and in serious need of a brush-through.

'So, are you going to tell me what's going on? Sometimes it's better to talk to a stranger than a friend.'

Suzie huffed. 'I can count the number of friends I have on one hand.'

Ryan felt sorry for her. 'That can't be right.'

'Look, I'm sure you know who I am . . . '

'Yes, I've read your books, and I'm sorry about last night,' he said sheepishly.

'I should have looked. My head was all over the place.'

Ryan crossed his legs and leaned back into the chair. 'I'm waiting.'

'I guess it started a while ago, when my laptop got stolen. I'd had a party, and I think that it was the day after, when I was at work in the card shop, I was burgled.

My story was on the laptop, but the editor already had it — so did I, once I got a new computer and downloaded it again. Unfortunately I had another story on there, unfinished, which was to be part of a series of romances in a small town. Melissa came out with her version six months after mine hit the shelves.' Suzie played with her hair, as she always had done when she was nervous.

'Then yours was the original?'

'Yes, but when it went to court she won. Apparently she had the work on a laptop, and could prove when it was written.'

Ryan stared out of the window and looked down into the street. He was trying to remember what happened when you saved something — could the history of the document be found? 'I'm not sure if it can be done, or if I've made this up, but I'm almost positive that you can get original time and date information from a document. Even if it has been saved afterwards.'

'Well, that wasn't done . . . and the laptop had a flower on the bottom. You know, in invisible ink.'

'I take it they didn't check that either?'

'No.'

Ryan looked at Suzie. She seemed tired and stressed. He had no idea how meeting someone could produce feelings in him almost immediately.

'So, then,' he said, 'all we can do is try and steal the laptop back, and find someone who is a techno whiz.'

'We don't know who stole it.'

'I have a fair idea who stole it,' he replied.

Her shoulders drooped. 'Come on, Ryan, how are we going to do that? Besides, how can I explain Crystal's manuscript being found here?'

Ryan watched her facial expression change from sad to thoughtful.

'The manuscript they found . . . ' She played with the duvet. ' . . . there were no red notes on the first page.'

'I don't get you.' Now he was lost, swimming in the ocean.

'I looked at Crystal's manuscript. She asked if I would give it a read-over — she was writing a crime novel; I assume that not everyone hates me. Anyway, I made notes in red pen. Even the first page needed something changing. When the officers showed it to me, there was no pen on the front page.'

Suzie took out her mobile and the card that Bill had given her. 'Bill, it's Suzie Cail. I know this is a big ask . . . That manuscript DI Tay has, can you see if there any notes in red pen on it?' She thanked him and then finished the call. All she could do now was wait.

8

'What I really want to know is, who killed Crystal and why.' Suzie walked towards the door. 'Are you coming? Or are you planning on sitting in that chair all day?'

Ryan's mouth twisted into a bit of a smile. He got up all the same and followed Suzie out of the door and into the street.

'You realise this is a strange way to have a date?'

'Who said I wanted to have a date with you?' Suzie tried to hold back her laughter; he was a really good-looking lad, and she would have been crazy to turn him down. 'So, why does your dad want to build a big monstrosity here, anyway?'

'He owns most of the land. My father is a bully, Susie: he will do whatever he can to intimidate people into agreeing with him.'

When they reached the bar, Suzie

leaned over and shouted, 'Des, do you need me?'

'Nah, you go and walk out with Ryan.'

Walk out? What on earth was that meant to mean? 'Des, I won't be long. I will help when I get back.'

'Fish and chips for tea.'

Ryan pulled her sleeve. 'What does he mean, 'fish and chips for tea'?'

'I've been helping him instead of doing the festival. He gives me free meals in return.'

'Seems fair.'

Suzie was thoughtful. She had heard about this golf course thing — not that she paid much attention to local gossip. Yet Des seemed to be all right with Ryan, as did several other people in the pub. They obviously didn't think badly of the son, even if the father was on the hit list of many of the local residents.

'I'm nothing like my dad, I hope you know that,' he said as though he could read her mind.

'I never said you were. Ryan, I don't even really know you, so how can I make a snap judgment after about an hour in each other's company?'

Suzie waited for the answer that she was sure was going to come, but instead he went to being all moody.

He sighed heavily. 'I'm sorry. It's just that I am so used to people having a dig at my dad that I jump first. He never listens to me anyway, so I just let him keep doing what he is doing. You know, I once tried to torpedo this stupid golf course plan when he first suggested it.'

'What happened?'

'He said I can either shut up or put up; my other option was to move out.'

She watched his reaction, his shoulders drooping. It didn't seem fair that his dad had said that. Families should stick together and not fall out over silly things. But she agreed with him: Castle Cove was too nice a place to destroy.

'You didn't move out?'

'No, to be honest. I can't afford to if I want to keep up the lifestyle.'

Suzie was shocked. 'Money isn't everything.'

Was Ryan some sort of money-grabbing idiot? Or just too used to having everything laid on a plate for him? People like that drove her crazy. Not everyone was lucky enough to have options: most people worked whatever job they could to bring in money.

Suzie decided that a change of subject was called for. 'Can we talk to that librarian?'

'Laurie? Why?'

'Because I want to know if they have a photocopier at the library; and, if so, who used it last.'

Ryan gave her a quizzical look, but said yes. They turned back at the lighthouse and made their way in companionable silence towards the library. For once, the sign on the door said 'Open'. He held the door for her in a gentlemanly gesture Suzie thought it was cute. It wasn't often that she was treated like that.

Laurie was sitting behind the counter, her back to the door.

'Hey Laurie, can I ask you something?'

She spun around on her chair. 'Sure, Ryan.'

'Do you have a photocopier here?'

'Yes. Do you need to use it?'

'Oh, no; I just wanted to know who has used it last.'

Laurie looked at Ryan, and then to Suzie, which made her feel very uncomfortable. 'Let me check.'

Laurie grabbed an old blue book from the desk and flicked through it. 'Melissa Spencer, she came in the other day to do some printing. Quite a lot, actually — she paid ten pounds in total. It's five pence per sheet.'

Why would anyone do such a large amount of printing when she wasn't a resident? Most manuscripts were sent via email these days. Few publishers still wanted them by post.

'You're that plagiarist Suzie Cail, aren't you?'

'My name is Suzie Cail, yes. But I am not a plagiarist.'

'Well, that's not what I read in the papers. You should count yourself lucky that you are even here,' Laurie replied. 'I wish you hadn't come. You've ruined my festival, and an innocent girl is dead — by your hands. It's hard to understand why the police let you, a killer, go. It's beyond me.'

Suzie wanted the ground to swallow her up. For months she had dealt with this sort of attitude, and it was getting tiring very quickly.

'Really, why would I kill my friend? Who the hell made you the judge, jury and executioner?' Suzie hadn't realised just how bad small towns were when it came to making the wrong assumptions about people.

'If the shoe fits . . . '

'Come on, Suzie, we need to go.'

'I would have thought better of you, Ryan, going with someone like that.'

'Who I go out with or don't go out with isn't your concern, Laurie.'

Suzie's blood was close to boiling point. Laurie had already made it clear on the first day that she wasn't welcome. With this exchange, she had just made her mind up for her. She exited hurriedly, Ryan following.

'Who's Melissa?' he asked when they were outside.

'The author I was telling you about. I

think she was the one who stole my work. It doesn't seem right that she was photocopying two hundred pages of — what?' Suzie sat on the pavement, her head in her hands.

'Suzie, are you okay?'

Tears fell onto the floor. She had come here to get away from all the hurtful comments, and here she was getting a load of aggravation — first from Melissa, then the police, and now Laurie. 'I'm fine,' she managed to say in between the sobs.

After a while her crying subsided. Taking a handkerchief out of her pocket, she wiped her eyes. 'Ryan can you do something for me? I want you to talk to Melissa Spencer. Then tell me what she knows.'

'What are you going to do?'

'I will get cleaned up and help out behind the bar, see if I can overhear any conversations. Crystal didn't know anyone here, so why was she killed?'

Suzie had so many questions regarding Crystal's death. She hoped Bill would get back to her soon.

Ryan said his goodbyes and walked off in search of Melissa Spencer. He was certain that she would be staying in the only hotel in town, which he wasn't looking forward to entering. He and Colin Michaels hadn't really got on since high school, and with his dad and Colin's grandmother at odds, things had got worse.

The hotel was only half a mile up the road, which was unusually quiet for this time of day. There was no one around; even the seagulls had flown off somewhere.

Suzie was a nice girl — or she seemed to be; Ryan paid little attention to rumours, and had read her book prior to it being pulled from the shelves. He'd thought it was very good; but then again, he was just one reader.

Ryan took a deep breath, flinging open the door to the hotel. Colin was stood behind the reception desk messing around with paper.

Is this what hoteliers do? Play with

paper whilst everyone else works? Ryan gave himself a mental shake; he was being mean, and Colin hadn't even said anything yet.

'Ryan, what do you want?'

'Look, Colin, I'm not involved in my father's plan.'

Colin raised his eyebrows, tutting. 'So, what do you want?'

'I need to know if Crystal left the hotel last night.'

'Why do you need to know? Hasn't that author been charged with murder?' Colin asked.

'No, she hasn't, and she is innocent.'

'So, let me guess, you're trying to be the knight in shining armour?'

'Come on, Colin, can't you put the aggro to one side? Is it fair an innocent person is being accused of murder?'

Ryan saw Colin's face change. He had always been sweet and kind when he was a kid. Ryan was the tough one, and so he didn't like him in high school; then, when his dad came up with that hare-brained scheme, everything changed.

'No. Are you sure she's innocent?'

'Yes, I am sure,' Ryan replied.

'I'll sort out the CCTV and give you a ring. You'll have to give me your number.'

Ryan took a business card out of his pocket and handed it over. 'I'd appreciate it if it's sooner rather than later.'

He wasn't sure this had been what Suzie was implying. Maybe it had merit. But if it meant another date with her — a proper one this time — then he would do whatever it took to seal the deal. *Ryan, you sound too much like your dad!*

He would need his car if he was going to hunt out Melissa. She could be anywhere. Or had she gone into Weymouth?

9

Suzie headed back to the pub. She'd decided somewhere along the road that she would help Des, and it would give her a chance to talk to Jamie and see if she had seen anything after she left work. The thought of investigating the murder herself had crept up on her whilst the police was interviewing her.

Several people were crowded outside the pub smoking cigarettes, whilst others struggled to get past them all, trying to get in.

One man in particular caught her attention. He was wearing torn jeans and one of those lumberjack-style shirts that had been popular in the nineties. He looked over at her, his face full of contempt. 'We don't need murderers here.'

Suzie thought it best not to respond, just in case it exacerbated the problem. Instead, she held her head high; yanking the door open, she stepped inside. The pub itself seemed fairly quiet; perhaps people were still over at the library in the upstairs rooms, or at the hotel listening to a talk, or something.

A few people were using the pool tables. A lady with salt-and-pepper hair sat at one of the tables alone. Suzie wandered over to her. 'Can I get you anything?'

'No thanks, love.'

'I can't help but notice you look unhappy. Oh, I'm Suzie, by the way.'

'I'm Mrs. Ainsworth, but you can call me Meg.'

'Well, Meg, how about I get us both a drink, and then you can tell me what's wrong?'

Meg nodded. Suzie hated to see anyone upset and if talking to a stranger helped then it was the least she could do. She walked over to the bar. 'Jamie, love, would you make us a pot of tea please.'

'Hey, Suzie. Sure, I'll bring it over.'

'Thanks, hun.'

More people started entering the pub, and Suzie was hoping that she and Meg would become invisible. Meg looked so despondent. 'What's wrong?' Suzie asked, concern etching her voice.

'Unless you know how to stop hate mail, I'm not sure how you can help me.'

Someone was sending this sweet lady hate mail? 'Why would anyone send you that?'

'I own Michaels' Hotel, along with my grandson — well, he will own it outright when I've gone. We own the land right up to the lighthouse, as well as halfway down in the other direction. I'm not sure you have been that far. Anyway, we have it open-access, for anyone to come and go. We were recently informed by a group of London solicitors that it's in the way of the new hotel-cum-golf-course.'

Meg paused for a minute and then continued. Suzie thought it was best not to interrupt.

'I thought the mail was because I stopped someone doing one of those underground basement thingies that are all the rage.'

'I've heard of people doing them in

London — so many problems messing with the foundations. I've heard that if they're done wrong, then the whole building can come down,' said Suzie.

'That was my point exactly. Then I thought it was because I voted for the literary festival. I think the festival is a wonderful idea, a great thing for our town. So many people . . . you know, we are booked solid. I think even Mrs. Henderson has taken someone in. Sort of an unofficial B&B — but don't tell anyone, she could get into so much trouble.'

'I can understand that someone somewhere is disgruntled . . . but hate mail? It's so out of fashion, at least in my book. But some people still say no smoke without fire.'

Meg shrugged. 'I voted against the golf course. That's when the letters started; I have a feeling that it is one member of the town council who is rather disgruntled. My grandson told me I should ignore it, but it's hard.'

Suzie could understand. The hate she had faced had been bad enough, but Meg seemed such a nice woman. 'Have you thought of going to the police about the notes?'

'Bill is such a sweet young man: I wouldn't want to bother him. Did you know I used to change his nappies?'

'No, really?'

'Yes, I knew his mother: we lived next door to each other for a while. Before she moved into Weymouth itself.'

'That's a shame. Don't you see your friend often these days?'

'No, we are too busy with the hotel, and Colin could do with more help. We seem to find staff hard to get.'

'I can try and find out who is sending you hate mail. My friend died, and I'm trying to do two things at once.'

'There's no harm in trying, I suppose,' Meg said as she took a sip of tea.

'I can't promise anything; but hey, I can try. I like your cardigan, by the way.' *Maybe you shouldn't say that, Suzie.*

'Thank you, I knitted it myself.'

Suzie absentmindedly put another spoonful of sugar into her tea.

'It's a shame that you will be going

home to London. I could teach you how to knit.'

'I may not be going home, I may be staying here. There's a cottage that I like the look of, and I'm hoping Des over there will give me some work.'

Meg's eyes sparkled with mischief. 'Well, we could do with a good receptionist, if you're interested — and you can always work and write at the same time.'

'I don't write,' Suzie replied harshly.

'Oh, yes you do. You can't fool me. Besides, what is your detective called again?' Meg put her hand up. 'No, now don't tell me . . . '

Suzie sat looking around her. Des had switched the television on over near the pool tables. The noise level had risen.

'I know who he is — DI Holland,' Meg said with a smile.

'Yes, you're right. I won't be writing any more of those.'

'Why ever not? You have the perfect crime to use, too. That young lass that was murdered, hate mail, and that golf course.'

Suzie smiled back indulgently. It was obvious that no matter what she said to Meg, it would go over her head. There was merit to what she had said. If she herself hadn't been angry about losing her new friend, then she would have considered it — but who would buy from her? Publishing is a fickle friend. One day, maybe.

Suzie still hadn't been over to Weymouth to see if they had a Dictaphone or some such recording device. The smaller, the better. She doubted anyone would be happy to be recorded.

'Suzie, are you alright?'

'Yes, sorry; I was just thinking. I need to go into Weymouth. You don't want to see your friend, do you?'

'It's getting late. Why on earth — ?'

'I need a small recording device.' *Why are you telling her about that?*

'I have one of those at the hotel. It's a pen one with a USP on it.'

Suzie laughed loudly. 'Don't you mean a USB?'

'Aye, that's it. I knew it was something like that. I usually leave all that techy stuff to my grandson.' Meg picked up the teapot, poured the last of the tea into their cups, and then made a face. 'Look, how about you come to mine and I will get you that recorder thing? Not sure what you want it for, but I can make us a sandwich and a better brew than this.'

Cautiously, Suzie looked around the pub. She didn't see the police or Melissa. 'Sure, lead the way, Meg. Where do you live?'

'In the little cottages — it's not far.'

Right, that was really helpful; there were so many pretty little cottages in Castle Cove. 'Is there one near the end of your row for sale?' Suzie asked as they exited the pub together.

'Yes, it's a sweet little cottage. Ethel used to live there; she was part of the breakdance team.'

Suzie gasped. 'Breakdancing?' So how did that fit?

'When the community centre needed a new roof a few years ago, we thought of ways we could raise the cash. We came up with sponsored breakdancing — keeps us fit. The team in Weymouth and ours have dance-offs every few months.'

'I'm impressed.' She was, but the talk was going further and further away from her investigation. Had Ryan got any further than she had?

They continued for a while in silence, before Suzie asked, 'Have you got any of those letters still?'

'Yes, but I'm not sure what good they will do. I haven't been to the police, as I can't see them being able to help. It's just someone sending notes — how would they be able to do anything?'

'We'll sort it, Meg,' Suzie replied, patting the woman's hand.

They arrived at the row of little cottages, all with uniform doors and windows. The only differences Suzie could see were the flowers which grew in the small front gardens. The one on the end was for sale: it was precisely this row of cottages Des had told her about. It was well within Suzie's price range — *well, it would be if I sold my London flat*, she thought to herself. Walking Meg home would afford her a look inside, though Suzie wished that the cottages were a little different from each other.

'I notice that they are all the same on the outside . . . ' she said enquiringly.

'Yes, it was something that the council in eighteen-hundred-and-whatever decided. I wish I could paint my door from white to a nice eggshell blue.'

Meg looked wistful. Suzie felt rather sorry for her.

When the front door finally opened and Meg moved aside to allow Suzie to gain access, she was surprised to see that the house was fairly minimalist — except for a lot of snow globes on the mantelpiece, depicting various places around the world.

'I'll just get you those letters,' Meg said, leaving her standing in the living room.

Walking straight into the living room through the front door wasn't something Suzie really liked. Perhaps there was enough room to build a little porch inside?

Meg handed over a few of the letters and the USB recorder. Suzie gave them a once-over. They were printed on heavy, expensive-looking paper. ''Vote *for the golf course or I will torch your hotel.*' These are really nice — not! Meg, try not to worry. I need to go, but I will be back.' Suzie turned to face the door, but then swung around. 'Will you be okay on your own?'

'Of course! Nothing has happened yet,' Meg said with a smile.

At least she wasn't letting it show that she was bothered, even though she probably was. Apart from keeping Meg company for a while, Suzie was getting nowhere fast. Perhaps it had been a bad idea. What had even convinced her that she could discover who had killed Crystal? Who knew? There was nothing she could do about it now; she was in too deep to walk away.

'Can I take these?' Suzie held up the sheaf of letters.

'Sure,' Meg said, shrugging her shoulders.

'I'd best get off. I need to go back to work, unless Des has decided he no longer requires me.'

'Pop round anytime. I'm usually either

here or at the hotel.'

'Of course I will.' Suzie smiled; at least she seemed to have made another friend here, one who didn't seem to mind her nefarious reputation.

Suzie arrived back at the pub after only a few minutes. 'Des, I'm just going to change my shoes.'

'Okay, lass. Hurry up, I could really use a hand.'

Suzie dashed up the stairs. There went her idea of spending time thinking things over.

* * *

Laurie stood by the bar, watching Suzie Cail disappear upstairs. She should really go and talk to her, but she wasn't sure if the woman really was blameless. People, especially here, assumed that you were guilty until proven innocent . . . Instead of going upstairs to see Suzie, she left her drink on the nearest table and escaped to the sanctuary of her library.

Laurie had been so happy that the literary festival was going well, and now this would put a blot on the whole thing. People would think that she had planned all this — a real murder to put Castle Cove on the map. Laurie braced herself: the questions would come, and she would need to answer them. She didn't really know what to do: the festival attendees couldn't leave Castle Cove. Until then, they would think of other things to do. The last talk was meant to be today, and then tomorrow would be a quiz of some sort.

A small queue had formed outside the library. Laurie had forgotten that she should have opened up today. 'How are you doing, Mr. Reed? I've got those new westerns in for you.'

Mr. Reed was a hero in her eyes, one of the last remaining members of the Second World War's Desert Campaign. 'Thanks, young 'un. You know, I don't know what I would do without the library.'

It was people like Mr. Reed that made running the library worthwhile. If only she could get the children absorbed in books instead of sitting down and playing

10

The car was heading straight for Laurie. Jumping out of the way, she fell hard onto the road. Tarmac dug into her leg, leaving her with a huge graze dotted with tiny stones. Shakily, she got up and hurried home. Why would anyone want to hurt her? Had she imagined it?

Once inside she got out her medical box, taking out gauze and pair of tweezers, and filling the washing-up bowl, adding a little Dettol to the water. Laurie cleaned her wound; it was really sore, and she wanted to scream as she used cotton wool to wipe it.

After she was sure the graze was clean, Laurie made a cup of tea and took it up to bed. The festival was going well, everyone knew what they were doing and she wasn't needed. Quiz night tonight; but after nearly being run over, she wasn't planning on going out again. She knew that wasn't possible, though, and would still go out tomorrow.

She snuggled down and went to sleep, her dreams filled with the oncoming car and her falling hard onto the road.

★ ★ ★

Suzie dashed back down to the bar and set to work. 'Des, do you want me to replace the optics?'

'Nah, lass. You take over from me, and I'll go and get some more bottles.'

'Okay.' The bar wasn't that busy, so Suzie took her chance. 'Jamie, I don't suppose you saw anything last night?'

'No, my boyfriend picked me up and we went off to his flat. It's out on the way to Weymouth. Not much out there, just a few flats and houses dotted along the main road, like. Sorry I can't help.'

Suzie was surprised that she didn't ask what this was about. 'What can you do around here?'

Jamie laughed. 'Planning on moving?'

'I've been thinking about it. I wouldn't be able to get these views in London.'

'That's true,' Jamie said, as she put

clean glasses on the shelves.

A customer interrupted them. 'Pint of your best bitter, please.'

Suzie poured the pint, took the money and threw it in the till.

'I heard you were arrested?'

'Yes. Apparently DI Tay thinks I killed Crystal Siena.' Suzie tried her best not to cry; she had done so much of that.

Suzie continued serving the customers, many of whom she didn't know. The festival was coming to a close, and the main murder mystery event was two nights away. Everyone would then head off in their own directions, which gave her only two days to figure all this out.

'So, do you know much about this golf course thing?'

'Oh, that's Mr. Arnley's doing,' Jamie said as she wiped the bar. 'He wants to buy the land surrounding the lighthouse and Michaels' Hotel.'

'Mrs. Ainsworth wouldn't sell. Not at all — even from my short acquaintance with her, I know that.'

'No, that she wouldn't.' Jamie poured them both a shot. 'Problem is that Mr.

Arnley hates taking no for an answer. You've been seeing a lot of his son.'

The penny finally dropped. 'Ryan,' Suzie said, aghast. 'He's never given a name to his dad, but he did say about the golf course.'

'They are the richest family in Castle Cove. Ryan is a decent lad, but seems not to have too much get-up-and-go. Under his father's thumb, so to speak.'

'Does he live with them?'

'I've not heard otherwise,' Jamie said, before she walked away and began serving customers that had started to queue up again.

Nothing Jamie had said contradicted what Ryan had told her earlier. A niggling doubt surfaced. Had Ryan planted the manuscript in her room? But then why would he have killed Crystal? No, that didn't make sense! The last thing she wanted to do right now was serve behind the bar; she had too many things to do.

'What do you know about Laurie?'

'Laurie Forster?' Jamie repeated the name. 'She is a bit of a strange one, fairly quiet. The library is her life, and she is fighting Mr. Arnley tooth and nail to stop him. Laurie is on the town council, but I'm not sure what good she will do.'

'Maybe I should talk to her.' Suzie wasn't really talking to Jamie, more to herself.

'Yes, you should. I'm sure she can clarify whatever it is you want to know.'

Suzie wondered if Crystal had had any enemies in the writing community. There were some who loved nothing better than to drag you down. Melissa was one example: she would talk about you behind your back. Because you didn't know the ones she spoke to, then you were made out to be the evil one.

Suzie's pocket vibrated. Taking out her mobile, a number she didn't recognise flashed on the screen.

'Hello!'

'Suzie?'

'Yes,' she replied.

'It's Bill. I checked the manuscript from DI Tay and it doesn't have any red pen on it. We couldn't find any clear fingerprints on it. Suzie, you need to stay away from DI Tay, because he's still of the mind you killed Crystal.'

'Thanks, Bill. Whoever put that in my room knew exactly what you would think.'

After cancelling the call, she looked around. Des was nowhere to be seen. All Suzie wanted to do was get out of the pub.

Laurie had invited everyone here. She wondered if she would have a list of all those people who were attending the festival.

The only other person she needed to speak to was Mr. Arnley. If he was as rich as they said, then he would have expensive paper. Suzie allowed the thought to eat away at her.

'Hey, Suzie, can you grab some of the glasses off the tables?' Des shouted from the other end of the bar.

He'd appeared from nowhere: she had been serving behind the bar for hours and hadn't seen him. 'Sure thing, Des.'

'Once you've done that, you can get off for a bit if you'd like.'

'Yes, thanks Des. Do you have any idea where I can find Mr. Arnley?'

'You could try the houses on Millionaires' Row. It's the end house. You'll be lucky if you can get past the security gate.'

'Millionaires' Row?' she said, confused.

'If you go out towards Weymouth, you will see a row of about six houses close to the headland. Mr. Arnley's is the last house before you reach the headland. I'm sure Ryan would take you, lass.'

'Thanks Des, I wasn't sure he would. Doesn't seem like he has a great relationship with his dad.'

'That may be, but it's quite a walk. Better in a car than on shanks' pony.'

Des was still wearing that leather waistcoat and white t-shirt; he did seem really attached to them. He obviously wasn't one for keeping up with the latest fashions.

Walking off, she did as Des asked and collected all the glasses left lying around on the fireplace, wooden tables, and even on the pool table cloth. After stacking them in the dishwasher, she went upstairs to have a quick shower and change.

Taking out her notebook that she

always kept in a handbag, she made a few notes.

Letters to Meg.
A manuscript, without red markings
  on.
Crystal's murder.

Were the three things connected — or were they all different crimes, which just appeared to be linked?

Tucking her notebook into her jeans pocket she headed out, half-debating over phoning Ryan or just getting a local taxi over to Millionaires' Row. She could do with speaking to Mr. Arnley without his son present. Perhaps he would be more willing to tell her what she knew — or not, as the case might be.

When Suzie went downstairs she headed through the kitchen and out of the back door: she didn't want to see Ryan if he was in the bar waiting for her. Instead, she bumped into Melissa, who smiled sweetly at her.

'Suzie! Trying to avoid the police, are we? I did hear you got arrested.'

'I suspect the whole town knows. What do you want, Melissa?'

'Nothing, just waiting for a phone call from my editor.' Melissa wore a gypsy skirt similar to the one Crystal had. 'It is much quieter this side of the pub. I hadn't expected to see you at all; I thought you would be locked up in a cell.'

'So, are you going to tell me how you got Crystal's manuscript into my room?' Suzie mentally shook herself.

'I don't know what you mean.' Melissa gave her an *I don't know what you're talking about* look. 'Although perhaps you can help me get a manuscript of *mine* back. I let Crystal Siena read something of mine, just to show how much further she had to go before she is as good as me. The little witch died before she gave it me back. I had thought that you could ask your friends down at the police station.'

'Melissa, do your own dirty work. I will not, now or ever, do something for you.'

Suzie didn't wait for her to reply; instead, she walked off, and hoped that she would be able to flag a taxi down.

Why would Melissa give anyone a manuscript? One thing she did know about her was that before her one-book success, she would let anyone read her work. Then afterwards she wouldn't let anyone look at her work in progress. She had always thought that she was far superior to everyone else.

So her saying that she'd allowed Crystal to see her manuscript wouldn't make any sense. It went against her entire feelings on the subject. If only Suzie knew what manuscript she was talking about. Maybe Meg would let her go into Crystal's room — unless it was still a crime scene!

Suzie hailed a passing taxi.

'Miss, you need to be careful. Where'd ya need to go?'

'I need to go to Mr. Arnley's house. I'm just not sure of the address, other than that it's on Millionaires' Row.'

'Aye, I know where it is. Hop in — be there in a jiff.'

The taxi driver spoke just like Des. It made her smile: how some people made her feel like she belonged, and others just like Laurie thought she was just an outsider.

'What are you going out there for? Mr. Arnley isn't known for his social niceties.'

'Thanks; I think I will be all right. I just really need to talk to him about something.'

'Oh, aye, he's all for business. Just like he's trying to ruin this town.'

Before Suzie had a chance to reply they were passing huge houses set back from the road, uniformed metal gates separating the outside world from each inner sanctum. A high wall was also a major feature of the properties. What did you have to do to live here? she wondered.

'We're here, lass, do you want me to wait?'

Suzie turned to him and smiled. 'I'm not sure how long I am going to be.'

'Here's me card. Give me a ring if you need a lift back.'

She handed him a five-pound note and promised to call when she had done.

Suzie stalled getting out of the car; every nerve ending in her body jangled. She walked slowly towards the silver intercom strategically placed on the wall. Pressing the button, she waited for someone to answer. It crackled: 'Yes?'

'My name is Suzie Cail. I'd like to speak to Mr. Arnley.'

The unknown male voice went silent for a moment. 'Do you have an appointment?'

'No. But I won't take up much of his time. Five minutes is all I need.'

The gate slowly started to swing. Suzie jumped back, waiting for it to have fully opened before she walked up the driveway. She was filled with trepidation: would she get a nasty reaction, or would Mr. Arnley be helpful? Maybe she should have waited for Ryan to take her, so he could have smoothed over any wrinkles?

Yellow roses lined the path up to the front door. They looked pretty, but Suzie was of the mind that just because you *seemed* to have everything, didn't mean you actually *did* have everything. The white front door opened before she walked up to the end of the drive. Suzie took several deep calming breaths before she walked any further.

A small man appeared, in a black suit and sporting a bowtie. 'Yes,' he said in a rather snooty voice. 'Can I help you?'

'I'd like to see Mr. Arnley, please.'

'Do you have an appointment?'

Suzie looked at the floor and then back up at the man. 'No. But I only need five minutes of his time.'

'I am afraid he is rather busy at present.'

She turned to walk away. Maybe she would have been better coming with Ryan.

'Perhaps he has a few minutes. If you will come with me, I will ask.'

She followed him through the marble-floored hallway. The house screamed money. *How the other half live*, she thought to herself.

'Just wait here, please.'

She had been taken into a study. On the desk was an old letter rack containing stationery. Suzie waited until she couldn't hear footsteps anymore, then quickly grabbed a blank piece of paper. Folding it up carelessly, she thrust it into her back pocket.

A somewhat strange gentleman walked into the room. 'Yes? What do you want? I am rather busy.'

Suzie steeled herself. 'I want to know why you've been sending Meg Ainsworth threatening letters.'

'Well, if that silly woman would have sold me her hotel and land, I wouldn't have needed to.'

'Do your threats resort to murder?' Okay, so maybe she had overstepped the mark a little bit now.

'No, they do not. Nothing is worth spending twenty-five years in a small cell.'

'Just lay off Meg, or else you will have me to answer to,' Suzie snapped, and walked back the way she had come, slamming the front door behind her.

She leaned against the door, gasping for breath. She couldn't believe what she had just done. Ryan was going to be so angry that she had forced her way into his home and threatened his dad.

Jogging down the driveway, Suzie made the decision to walk further down the road before phoning the taxi. The less time she spent around Millionaires' Row, the better.

A car pulled up alongside her. 'Hey, Suzie, were you looking for me? You could have just phoned.' Ryan sighed indignantly.

'If you must know, I came to see your dad. I was sure the letters Meg had got were from him. Who else in this place can afford expensive paper like that?'

'I knew he had done it as soon as you showed me the letters. Look, he's a pathetic man who thinks all he can do is bully people. Are you getting in? Or are we going to air this in public?'

Suzie walked around to the passenger side, climbing in carefully. 'So why didn't you say anything?'

'What could I say?'

'The truth.' She sighed. 'Meg gave me some notes that she had received, threatening her, trying to make her vote for the golf course.'

'Do you have them with you?'

Suzie took them out of her small beaded bag. 'Yes, here.'

She watched with interest as Ryan

fingered the paper. Had he noticed the same thing she had, that the paper felt expensive? 'Have you any ideas?'

'What about the notes? Perhaps can I keep these? I will know more tomorrow.'

Suzie thought better of questioning him. Ryan knew more than he was letting on, she was sure of that.

'You may think I have money — and yes I have a flashy car, but I don't actually own anything.' Ryan drummed his fingers on the steering wheel.

'You know that noise is annoying.'

Ryan gripped the steering wheel so hard his knuckles turned white. 'Why didn't you tell me you were coming? My father is unpredictable and can turn nasty in an instant. You could have been hurt.'

'Ryan, I'm sorry. I just couldn't see Meg frightened anymore. It isn't fair, she doesn't deserve that.'

'I know, and I've tried to get him off the idea of ruining the town. I did have a small idea that maybe he would be satisfied with just a nine-hole golf course, instead of the huge eighteen-hole one he's planning. There's a disused factory not far away — he could use that land.'

'That's a great idea!' Suzie squealed. 'Maybe you could talk with him about it?'

'Yes. I'll drop you back in town, then see what he says.'

'Thanks, Ryan. I didn't mean to cause you any aggravation.'

'You didn't.'

Ryan stopped the car. Turning to face her, he leaned over and brushed his lips gently against hers. 'You know, once this is all out of the way, then maybe I can take you out on a proper date. Without you running around trying to find a killer.'

'Well, is it my fault that the facts didn't seem to add up? It's all a jumbled mess.' Suzie felt like she was hunting for a needle in a haystack, and Ryan was being too much of a distraction for her.

'I just know my dad. No matter how ruthless he is in business, he wouldn't kill anyone.'

11

Ryan woke to the sound of his phone ringing. Bleary-eyed, he reached for it. 'Mmm?'

'Ryan, it's Colin. I've dug out that CCTV footage, and I think you need to get over here and have a look.'

Ryan was still half-asleep, not sure whether he was dreaming or if he was actually talking to a real person on the phone. 'Yes, yes. I'll be there.' He hung up and snuggled back down under the duvet.

He fell back asleep for a while, but woke with a start. *Colin called, didn't he?* Or had he only been dreaming that his phone had rung? He picked up the mobile from his bedside table and checked the call log. Yes, Colin had rung, and Ryan had said that he would go and see him.

Ryan dressed quickly, grabbing his car keys. He dashed to Michaels' Hotel.

When he arrived there was a crowd of people outside, all jostling each other. He wondered what was going on, but then he saw the journalists stood in front of the hotel. The crowd was either watching the show, or they had been questioned by the wonderful press.

He walked around the back of the crowd and through the doors. Ryan couldn't believe how much this murder had affected the town. For years he had hoped something exciting would happen, but never had he thought for one moment it would be something like this.

Colin was sat at the reception desk, talking on the phone. Looking up, he mouthed that he would be with Ryan shortly.

Ryan sat on one of the leather chairs and waited patiently. Had something been mentioned about CCTV? Perhaps it was something that Suzie was adamant about. Something was strange about the whole business.

When Colin got off the phone, he shouted over, 'Ryan, come into the office.'

Ryan got up and followed him. One

thing was certain — Colin didn't have to do any of this.

'Look, I found something. I'm not sure how significant it is, and I haven't shown the police yet, although I should.'

'I'm glad you called. So what is it?'

'Okay. I checked all the night's footage.' Colin put a video cassette in the machine and pressed play.

Ryan watched with bated breath. On the screen, Crystal walked out of the hotel grounds, a brown envelope in her hands. It looked a little bulky to be just a letter.

'If you look at the time, Crystal leaves the hotel at midnight. Although no one remembers her going.'

'If you have someone on reception all the time, wouldn't they have seen something?' Ryan found it perplexing that someone could just get past the front desk without being seen. 'Is there a back door that your guests can use to leave?'

'Nope, they are only allowed to come and go through the main entrance. I'm sorry it doesn't tell you much. I have checked every tape since the start of the festival.'

'Thanks, Colin. Have you shown this to the police?'

'No, not yet, but I can see you're worried. I remember the face you make.'

'Yes, you know me.' Ryan regretted the way things had turned out with Colin. They used to be friends, when they were kids.

'Not any more, I don't,' Colin said with sadness.

There weren't many young ones around Castle Cove, and they should really stick together. 'Well, maybe we can fix that. Have a game of pool one night, or something?'

Colin smiled. 'Yeah, I'd like that.'

'Thanks for looking up the footage for me. It's a date. We'll see if you can still beat my ass at pool.'

Colin laughed, and with that Ryan left. The camera crews had moved further down the road. Ryan jumped in his car and drove around town: today, more than any other day, it felt small. *Too small.* Should he escape? Castle Cove held nothing for him, and Ryan knew he had ostracised most of his old friends. Those that he hadn't, had moved away as soon as they could.

Without any money of his own, moving wasn't a possibility. He'd look for a job that paid well, and to hell with his dad's company. He'd speak to his dad when he got home. Ryan knew as soon as he had seen the notes who had written them; it didn't take a genius to spot that.

Instead of going over to the Castle Arms, Ryan turned his car around and headed home. The view over the cliffs was gone before he could really drink it in. Those were a few good things about Castle Cove: the views, the fresh air and the long cliff walk to the lighthouse. The freedom . . . if he went to a city, he would feel hemmed in. Ryan felt that he couldn't win no matter what he did.

Using his fob, he opened the gates to the house, zipping up the driveway. *I should have checked the post box*, he remembered — but this was too important to bother with small things like that.

His dad's Jaguar was sat in the

driveway; Ryan took several calming breaths before he got out of the car and entered the house.

'Dad! Dad! Where are you?'

'Study!' a voice shouted back.

Ryan strode into the study. His dad was sat in his leather chair, wearing shorts and a sleeveless top. 'See you've changed out of your suit,' he said angrily.

'Not that comfy to sit in, is it?'

'Dad, I want a word with you.' Ryan took the chair opposite.

'Don't you take that tone with me, lad!'

'I'll take any tone I like with you, especially when you send threatening notes to a sweet lady. Why? Go on, tell me why!'

'Look, I've already had some young lass telling me off about that. Who the hell does she think she is?'

'You want to knock down her friend's hotel — what for? Just to build *another* hotel? And ruddy golf course?'

'It's none of your business what I do.'

'It is when I'm ostracised because of your business dealings.' Ryan stood up and paced the study.

'Who'd dare ostracise my son? Tell me and I will make them pay for it.'

Ryan was shocked; he'd never imagined his dad thought anything of him. 'Why do you care? You're not bothered about me.'

His dad's face fell and turned white. 'Is that what you think? No, lad, you have it all wrong. I would move heaven and earth for you. I love you.'

'I thought you hated me?'

'No, I'm so sorry that you ever thought that, Ryan. I know I keep myself busy and don't spend enough time with you. Since your mum died, work is all I think about. I miss her . . . but I forgot about you.'

Ryan stayed silent, trying to take in what had been said.

'This golf course plan was just another way to keep me busy. Otherwise I have nothing to do.'

Finally, Ryan spoke. 'Have you got a map of the town, Dad?'

'Yes, I have somewhere.' His dad threw open the drawers of his desk and rifled through them. 'You could try that cabinet over there. Why do you want a map?'

'Because I have just had an idea and I

need to see if it is possible.'

Ryan found a map folded away in the filing cabinet. Taking it over to the desk and laying it out, he pointed. 'Look at this. Do you remember the old biscuit factory? It has loads of land around it. Okay, so perhaps not big enough for an eighteen-hole golf course, but it is certainly big enough for a nine-hole.'

His dad bent his head over the map, studying it. 'Mmm. You know what, Son, I think you have a great idea. I may even be able to extend to the old warehouse building next door. I might get my eighteen-hole course after all.'

'If you did it this way, you wouldn't have to knock a hotel down to get what you want.'

'Here's the deal. Tomorrow I will phone up the council and see who owns those two properties, and if they're for sale then we're buying them.'

'We are?'

'Yes, if you'd like?' his dad said hesitantly. 'I want to work with you on this. I'm going to pay you a decent wage. I'm not sure I can make everything up to you, but I want to try.'

Ryan didn't cry under normal circumstances, but a single tear fell onto his cheek now. 'Yes, let's do this. But I do think you need to apologise to Meg. Sending those notes was downright nasty, even for you.'

'First thing in the morning, Son. First thing in the morning.'

Ryan smiled at his dad and left him to it in the study. He was glad his father had had a change of heart — but how long would it last? His dad had always had a nasty streak when it came to getting what he wanted. Only time would tell. He knew it would be hard to turn over a new leaf. Ryan just hoped that he would become a good businessman rather than a scheming, underhanded one.

Now he had one problem solved, but still had another — what about Melissa? He needed to get her to admit that she'd stolen Suzie's and Crystal's work. He had a recording device, so perhaps a little honey trap might be in order.

Ryan went into the kitchen for a drink. Flicking the kettle on, he sat at the breakfast bar and thought about how he could catch Melissa acknowledging what she'd done. Then everyone would know what a lying, scheming little witch she was.

12

Melissa sat on the beach, an old-fashioned Dictaphone in her hand. *'Cassy inched her way up the stairs, her eyes transfixed at the light above.'* She placed the top sheet on the bottom of the pile, and carried on reading the novel aloud, recording every word.

This was surely going to be another bestseller for her, and no one would be any the wiser about whose manuscript it really was. After all, the real author was dead, and she had told Melissa herself that no one else had seen the manuscript yet.

Melissa smiled. Then it hit her — what would she do after this? She knew deep down she was no writer, not without stealing ideas off other people. She was good at grammar, so silly people sent her their stories and she twisted them around into her own.

Mix and match a few story ideas

together, and they would never know that Melissa's story was actually theirs. She continued to read the manuscript until she had done it all, the warmth of the sun keeping her company.

This little cove she had found offered her privacy. Once she got back home, she would type it all up and send it off to her publishers. The manuscript she held in her hands would need to go. Damn; she had forgotten the one that the police had as evidence. Perhaps planting it in Suzie's room hadn't been such a good idea.

Gathering her things, Melissa headed back to her room. She had tired of the festival and all the talks. One good thing had come out of it — this. Possibly the book of the year. She also had several further ideas from listening to other people's plots.

Melissa knew she was good at integrating with people; she would drink and laugh with the rest of them. Suzie was very much a wallflower, preferring to stay at home rather than to be the centre of attention. She had seen her at parties, and quite often Suzie was standing alone, watching the crowd around her.

Melissa hadn't yet reached the top of the ramp, which led up from the cove to the street above, when she saw a hottie walk past. He had gone before she reached the top — that was a shame, she would very much have liked to get to know him better.

This book should get her a bit of attention. Maybe she would grab a television deal? Or even a much larger advance than the one she got now.

Once she was in the safety and security of her own room, Melissa decided to phone her publisher up. 'James? Hi, it's Melissa. I have a great story for you.'

'What kind of story? Because you really need to change it up a bit.'

'Yes, I have. It's a crime novel set in London. I think you will love it. Horses, carriages and murder.'

'Okay, sounds interesting. I want the first three chapters on my desk first thing Monday morning.'

'No problem, James.'

Melissa put the phone down. She

strode over to the mirror and smiled. This was going to be her big break.

13

Meg felt like a huge weight had lifted off her shoulders. Peering out of the window, she saw the sky was splattered with fluffy clouds. Although Colin knew about a few of the notes, she had received many more threatening ones. Colin worried enough about her, and he didn't need another excuse to insist she sold her cottage and moved in with him. Since she had spoken to Suzie, things seemed to feel so much better: a problem shared was a problem halved, and so forth. For months now she had expected someone to put her windows through, or to set fire to her precious hotel.

Yet nothing happened. The strange phone calls were a rarity now, and since the festival had started things had gone strangely quiet. *No, Meg, remember the note you got the day the festival started?* That was one that she'd given to Suzie, and hopefully that young girl would get to the bottom of it.

She had a quick wash and put on her running leggings. Not that she ran these days, but rather speed-walked around the headland. It was one of her only pleasures: she was bored with being an hotelier. Bored of breakdancing with the same few people. Bored of being alone as more and more people left the town. Meg felt that she was being left behind. Even her little cottage bored her; it had looked the same for years. Suzie was a breath of fresh air, and she hoped that the young girl would stay around. She had to admit that it was nice to see the town full and vibrant again.

Grabbing her keys off the bedside table she headed out of the door and crashed straight into Mr. Arnley. He was dressed in his usual red woollen suit and matching waistcoat. A golden watch chain hung from his waistcoat pocket. He looked like something out of the 1930s rather than 2018.

'Watch what you are doing, Mr. Arnley.'

'Just the woman I want to see.'

'Really. And what do you want now?' Meg wasn't best pleased to be accosted by such an arrogant, self-centred man as Mr. Arnley. And his son was such a sweet boy!

'I think we need to discuss the sale price of your hotel,' he said in a very snooty tone.

'My hotel isn't for sale. I don't know how many times I have to tell you. I think we have enough businesses in Castle Cove, and you need to get your head out of the sand. Especially if you think that you can bully all the citizens of this town.'

'You know I could contact Environmental Health and have you shut down.'

'Try it.' With that last retort, Meg sidestepped him and walked quickly away.

She was shaking with anger. How dared he say that he would have her business shut down? What would her poor Colin do? There weren't many jobs around, and most of those that were available were only seasonal. Meg considered what she would do as she made her way over the cliff edge towards Michaels'. *Honestly, that man will be the death of me!*

'Mrs. Ainsworth! Look, I'm sorry.'

Meg turned back round and watched a very unfit Mr. Arnley running to catch up with her.

'I have sort of changed my mind,' he explained, panting.

'Really? 'Sort of'?'

'Yes. I would still love to buy your hotel — it's a great business — but I accept you won't sell. I had a bit of help with my decision on what I will do next. I'm going to buy the old factory over on Tattersall Road, and turn that land into a golf course instead. I want to know if I have your support.'

Meg looked quizzically at him. 'Does this mean you will leave my hotel alone?'

'In part, yes. I was wondering if Michaels' would sponsor a golf match when the course first opens.'

'You send me nasty letters, make horrible phone calls, and hound me for months. Now you have decided that everything is going to be hunky-dory? So it's 'Let's be partners in a match'? If I didn't know any better, I would say you're drunk.'

'Meg, I'm sorry. Ryan has already hauled me over the coals for it. I've changed the course to a nine-hole instead of an eighteen. Rejuvenating the old biscuit factory.'

'Nothing you can say can make this all right. What you did was the lowest of the low.'

'I realise that, Meg, and I can only apologise and hope that you will forgive me. I just wanted to improve tourism, and hadn't thought of the impact it would have on everyone.'

'Oh, well that's all right then, isn't it?'

'Work is the only thing that keeps me going. Ever since Beth died, I've been lost. Almost lost my son because of it.'

May suddenly felt sorry for him. He had been wrong, and done wrong, but the look of sorrow and loneliness etched on his face made her anger crumble to almost nothing. Though it would take a while before she could forgive him.

'Have you any other plans?' she asked, more politely now.

'Well, there is another warehouse that I could buy, and maybe turn into a play centre for the kids with a crazy golf course. You know the sort of thing — they buy a wristband and they can use the arcade games all day without paying anything else. I had thought of doing a go-kart track as well.'

'Would there be room for all that?'

'I'm not sure. Perhaps you would like to help me? I know it is a big ask, and . . . '

'I'll think about it.' She touched his arm. Perhaps she wasn't going to be bored after all. Not that she would give him her answer yet — no harm in making him grovel a bit more.

Mr. Arnley tilted his hat at her, and May was left standing on the cobbled path. She was shocked. Never in her thirty years of their acquaintance had he apologised. She wouldn't hold her breath that he would do it again. But the new plan to turn the biscuit factory into a golf course had merit. Plenty of space. Tourists might come and book her hotel out for several weeks of the year. Yes, Meg thought, it definitely had potential, and she could quite happily support it.

If only he hadn't done what he did. It would take time for her to forgive him, but she had no doubt she would eventually. May didn't like falling out with people — life was too short for that. And Mr. Arnley could be a handsome man, if only he would change out of that horrid suit. Next time she saw him, she would suggest a change of outfit, and he could take or leave her advice.

★　★　★

Suzie walked along the beach towards the broken ladder that went down from the cliff top to the sand. She took a long, hard look at it, having never really noticed the ladder from the beach before. Erosion had diminished the steel. A few rocks sat at the bottom, as if they had been placed there. Would Crystal have climbed down there? It seemed a little too unsafe — even Suzie wouldn't have, and she wasn't scared of heights.

The cliffs showed signs of the erosion which made many areas of Castle Cove headland dangerous too close to the edge.

Suzie knew that this was a typical effect of the sea reclaiming the land. Yet no barriers had been put into place to protect walkers.

Crystal had been found face-down in the sea, but she had not been killed without putting up a struggle. If nothing else, Suzie was determined to get justice for her friend. Crystal hadn't, Suzie decided, been above the beach, so the only other logical explanation was that she'd been talking a walk along the shore.

The newspapers and news channels were having a field day; they had descended on the town like locusts. If the town hadn't been packed before, it certainly was now. She struggled to get a meal even at the Castle Arms — she didn't want to put Des out, so had taken to buying fish and chips most days.

What was it that Sherlock Holmes said? 'When you have eliminated the impossible whatever remains, however improbable, must be the truth.' So all she had to do was eliminate the impossible.

Suzie looked up and saw Mathew, Crystal's ex, nearby, staring into space.

She jogged towards him. 'Mathew, can I have a word?'

His hands were jammed in his pockets, and he didn't seem to hear her. 'Mathew?'

'Sorry, I didn't see you.' Mathew looked crestfallen, and heavy dark shadows decorated his eyes.

'Mathew, could I ask you something?'

'I guess. Do your worst.'

'You argued with Crystal several times before her death. Could I ask why?' Suzie didn't take her eyes from his. Mathew rubbed his face before turning to face the sea.

'I'd borrowed money from people who you should never borrow from. They put the frighteners up me. I needed to pay them off quick. I lost the love of my life because of the way I am with money.'

'My gran used to say, *neither a borrower nor a lender be.*'

'Sound advice. I wanted Crystal back, but I knew that unless I sorted myself out, then I would never have her.'

'I'm sorry, Mathew,' she replied, not really knowing what to say.

'It's my fault I got in debt; my fault she's dead. It's all my fault.'

'No, Mathew, it wasn't your fault. Yes, borrowing money from loan sharks or gangsters definitely wasn't a bright move. But Crystal's death had nothing to do with you.' Suzie was sure that he was innocent of the murder: it was clear to see that he'd loved her. 'Crystal was a nice person.'

'You didn't know her.' Mathew turned on his heel and strode away.

Suzie was left standing, staring at the back of him whilst Mathew virtually ran away from her. It still didn't get her any closer to figuring out who would want Crystal dead.

Laurie had saved her precious library, if the rumours were to be believed, what with all the publicity around the festival thanks to the murder. Castle Cove was swarming with reporters and TV crews, and it was even harder to get into the restaurants and cafes now than it had been at the start of the festival.

Suzie took out her notebook and sat on a rock, jotting down her ideas. Crystal's manuscript was missing, and as far as the publisher knew, no one had seen it. It would be easy for the thief to pass off as their own if that was the reason for taking it.

Just like what had happened when her laptop had been stolen. Had Crystal owed money to people that she shouldn't have borrowed from? Just like Mathew did — but he loved Crystal . . .

Suzie, stop it! You are going around in circles.

What she could do with was going back to the beginning of everything.

Twelve months ago, her laptop had been stolen. Luckily, she'd had a back-up of her manuscript, but then Melissa came out with her own novel — actually Suzie's, virtually verbatim. But Suzie's own publishers hadn't supported her in court — another reason she'd lost. The laptop Melissa had stolen was produced as the thief's own. Suzie needed to get the laptop back, and then check out the hidden history files which most people assumed would be deleted.

It had been so obvious, staring her in

the face all the time: it had all started back then with one stolen manuscript and now two. Did Melissa steal the manuscript? And then, was it possible that Crystal had fallen over the edge of the cliffs accidentally? No, not that. It didn't happen; she didn't fall. *Tide charts are what I need. Now, where to get them?*

She spoke the last few words aloud, not realising someone was standing behind her. The figure stepped back into the shadows, hidden by a huge rock.

Suzie walked along the beach, kicking pebbles. So much didn't make sense, and she hated to admit that she didn't have a clue. Murders were what she *wrote*, with *fictional* detectives: it wasn't real life. This was.

Walking past the old broken stairs, Suzie paused and looked up: jagged rocks and a sheer drop. So Crystal must have been walking along the beach, not above on the cliff top. Melissa couldn't have seen her walking up there — but she could have seen her walking down below.

Suzie ran as fast as she could back to the Castle Cove library. She wanted to have a word with Laurie and see if she knew anything. Part of her realised that Laurie might not even be interested in solving the murder, as she had got what she wanted.

The library was safe, if the rumours were to be believed in the first place. She hurried quickly back up the ramp and towards the Castle Arms. There were a lot of people jostling each other on the pavements, and some visitors walking down the road. Suzie presumed that they would think it was a safer option. Dodging the cars seemed to be preferable to dodging the people.

Laurie Forster was nowhere to be found, and the doors to the library were locked. Suzie peered into the windows to see if she could spot her taking a break or sleeping on the job. Nothing; perhaps she was at home. Suzie didn't know where Laurie lived, and didn't feel like she could visit her there even if she had.

The sky had turned velvet black, and the sea was crashing against the shore. The whole town had taken on an eerie feel. *Perhaps the weather is showing its sorrow for the loss of Crystal? Maybe not — the weather doesn't have feelings. Don't be silly, Suzie.*

She walked down the little cobbled side street where the estate agent's was. At the end of the street stood two people hidden by the shadows. Suzie wondered what they were doing there, so out of the way. Putting them out of her mind, she looked in the window at the various houses for sale. There, taking centre stage in the window, was the little cottage along Meg's row — a house in a cul-de-sac near to the Castle Arms, which looked pretty and would need modernisation. Crystal would have loved a house like that.

After she took down the details of the house, Suzie hunted high and low for Laurie. No one had seen her. Wasn't she meant to be doing a quiz tonight? A quick check of her watch told her that if Laurie was going to be anywhere, then she would be at the pub by now.

Suzie jogged back to the pub. It was busy with people waiting for the quiz to start. Des was in his usual place behind the bar. 'Des, have you seen Laurie?'

'No. Apparently she's gone missing. No one has seen her since yesterday.'

Suzie thanked him and moved through the throng. Melissa was standing beside the whiteboard. Suzie tried to blend into the crowd behind her, straining to listen to the conversation.

'Oh, my publisher is going to love my new book.'

'What genre?' someone asked.

'It's a murder set in London. I'm so happy I came here, because I've managed to write loads.'

'I thought you wrote romances?' Suzie said snappishly.

'I do! My next book in the series is based in a wedding shop. I thought that I would have a change; everyone loves crime,' Melissa said, in a fake posh voice.

'Oh.'

'What? Don't be jealous, Suzie, it doesn't suit you. Just because I can write better fiction than you.'

'Really? I think we write the same — except your stories are first person, and mine are third person. You know, I really loved your books set in a small town . . . all your others have been set in big cities.'

'Well, you know what they say — a change is as good as a rest.' Melissa gave one of her fake smiles.

'Oh, Melissa. You must give me some advice, I can't believe how good a writer you are,' someone in the group surrounding them said.

'Of course, but I hope you're not like some guy I tried to help. He wrote a book but wouldn't take any advice. Obviously, he was paying me.'

'What happened?' said a guy in shades and a baseball cap.

'Oh, I told him I wasn't working for him anymore. I mean, if he can't take any advice, what is the point in me editing his work? Honestly, some people just cannot be helped,' Melissa said icily.

Suzie hated the smug way that Melissa went around telling people just how marvellous she was. There must be other people who hated the way she was: so fake. It was obvious to anyone that cared to watch her that she was a sneaky, nasty person. Besides, she also knew that there was no way Melissa or anyone could write fifty thousand words in a few days. Especially not here, when there were so many other things that you had to do.

A thought struck Suzie: had Melissa taken Crystal's manuscript, and then somehow planted it in her room when she was found dead? Or had it been done before that?

Suzie thought she was better off helping Des serve the scores of customers, instead of wandering around aimlessly looking for Laurie. She took her place behind the bar and served the hordes of tourists and locals alike.

Ryan came in, dressed all in black, looking very handsome. Perhaps he could be someone special? Someone she could spend a lot of time with?

'Hi, Suzie. What time do you get off?' Ryan asked her.

Suzie laughed. 'I'm not sure. Whenever Des doesn't need me. My stay is nearly over, and it's going to be sad to leave.'

'You can't leave, not now. Besides, we still have a murder to solve,' Ryan said, brushing her arm with his hand.

'I know, but then what?' Suzie had already planned to put in an offer on the little cottage; she just didn't want to say anything until it was all finalised.

'We can sort that. Have you heard what my dad has done?'

'No.' Suzie steeled herself for more of Mr. Arnley's antics.

'He's decided to buy the old biscuit factory and use that for his precious golf course. So the town is safe. I'm not sure how many people know yet, but they all should be happy. I will manage it for him, and earn a proper wage too.'

Suzie just smiled at him, warmth filling her insides. At least one thing has gone right.

'I think he has a soft spot for Meg, too. He's talking about taking her out for dinner as an apology.'

She raised her eyebrows and wanted to laugh — such a strange U-turn in such a short time! 'Well, we will just have to watch that space.'

'I sort of had it out with him. He's apologised for the way things are between us. Maybe things will be better from now on.'

'I hope so, Ryan. I have only known you for a few days, but I . . . ' Suzie didn't know what to say. She didn't want to appear needy for a new friend — or a . . . could she say *boyfriend*?

Suzie hoped so. She had discovered that he felt deeply about being ignored and feeling unloved. She leaned forward and whispered in his ear, 'I have an idea on how we can catch our killer, but I will tell you when it's a bit quieter. We need to find Laurie too.'

He nodded. 'Later, then.' Straightening up, he called across the pub: 'Des, fancy a game of pool? I'm not one for quizzes.'

'Sure — I reckon Suzie and Jamie can cope without me.'

Suzie just nodded before turning her attention to the queue of customers. The noise in the room was deafening; there were going to be a lot of people disappointed if Laurie didn't turn up to do the quiz.

14

Suzie went to help Jamie for a while whilst Des and Ryan were still playing pool. The quiz had been taken over by Mr. Joshua. Luckily, all the questions had already been left at the pub, along with the empty sheets for people to fill in. Suzie wanted to join in but she wasn't very good at general knowledge.

She decided to wait until the quiz was about to start, when everyone would be in their seats, drinks in hand. Once everything was underway, and she knew that she wouldn't be needed for a while, she made her escape.

Suzie made her way over to Michaels' Hotel. She wanted to know if she would be able to gain access to Melissa's room. Well, the woman should be kept busy for a while yet; she would never know that Suzie had been in.

The hotel stood alone and resplendent against the coastal backdrop. Its huge glass entrance doors reminded Suzie so much of the hotels in London. Her heart beat fast; she hoped that she wouldn't end up back at the police station by ten o'clock tonight.

She took several deep breaths before she walked through the doors. There was a fit young lad on reception, who seemed to be oblivious to her. Suzie walked slowly towards the desk, looking over her shoulder, half-expecting to see Melissa pop up behind her.

'Can I help you?' he asked, when he finally looked up from the computer.

'I'm looking into the death of Crystal Siena. I . . . I . . . wonder if I could get into Melissa Spencer's room.'

'I really shouldn't do that. It's against our privacy policy.'

Oh, that's right — hide behind the privacy policy line! Suzie thought to herself. The man went back to doing whatever he'd been doing on the computer before she came in. He was dressed in a black shirt that had a massive white collar on it. Weird dress sense; you couldn't help some people.

'Look, please ... my friend was murdered, and I'm just trying to find out what happened to her.'

At this, he turned back to face her, raising his eyebrows. Suzie could see that he was thinking about what she has said.

'Are you the police?'

'No, I'm not. Please — I would really appreciate it.' He was pretty cute. She waited with bated breath to see if he would allow her upstairs. Melissa could be back at any moment, and she was still stood at reception.

'Okay, you have five minutes. That's it.'

'Thank you. I didn't catch your name?'

'It's Colin. Follow me,' he said.

Suzie nodded, grateful he was letting her up, though he did seem rather sharp in the way in which he had spoken to her. The hotel looked just as good on the inside: leather sofas around glass tables. He guided her to the lift. They didn't speak. Suzie really had no idea of what to say. Colin kept his eyes staring at the lift door.

She was extremely thankful when the doors opened onto Melissa's floor.

'Her room's number six,' he said stiffly.

'I won't be long.'

'Oh, you won't be going in there alone. I'm coming in too.'

Suzie looked at him, exasperated. 'Okay.' She guessed that having him there would either prove or disprove her theory.

Melissa's room was a bit of a mess, with clothes dumped on the floor. A manuscript lay higgledy-piggledy on the dressing table. Suzie picked up a pencil off the side, and used it to lift the top pages, to check what the manuscript was. On one of the pages was a red mark, and on the bottom a note she had made for Crystal.

'Colin, you need to call the police. Now!'

'But . . . but . . . '

'Putting it bluntly, this is — '

'It looks like a pile of paper,' he said, pulling a face.

'No, this is Crystal Siena's manuscript — the one she was, I think, killed for.' Suzie gave him one of her black looks. She needed to impress on him that time was of the essence before Melissa came back to the hotel.

Suzie sat herself on the edge of the bed and thought for a moment. 'No, Colin — on second thoughts, don't tell anyone we have been here.' Taking out the camera in her jacket pocket, she took several pictures of the room and of the manuscript.

She smiled silently to herself. With Colin's testimony if necessary, they could say that they had found the missing manuscript. Suzie's name had already been blackened, and she would be damned if she would let it happen again. Perhaps this would be what she needed to clear herself — if, and only if, she could get Melissa to confess to stealing people's work.

Suzie knew she was still a long way from finding out who had killed Crystal. Even if she could prove the theft, it proved nothing else if nobody would listen.

'You finished now?' Colin asked suddenly.

He was stood with his hands in his pockets, looking very cross. 'Yes. Thanks,

Colin. Oh, before I go, do you know anything about those notes your grandmother has received?'

'Yes, but they're just hot air. Grandma worries too much.'

'Well, she seemed genuinely concerned about them.'

'Look, mind your own business. I will look after her; she doesn't need someone fuelling her fear.'

Suzie walked past him without saying another word. She didn't wait for him to shut the door, to chastise her anymore than he already had. Whoever sent those notes to Meg had certainly been in favour of the hotel-cum-golf-course.

Taking her phone out of her pocket, she sent a text to Ryan. She had no idea where he was or what he was up to. Hopefully he would be okay, considering there was a killer in Castle Cove.

★   ★   ★

Ryan had found Melissa sat in the café at the end of Bluebell Lane. He ordered a coffee. Whilst he waited, he looked around at which table would be nearest to her so he could hear what she said, if anything. A small table by the window was the only one close enough to her. Normally the café would have shut at six o'clock, but due to the festival it was closing at ten-thirty.

'There you go, dear.' Mrs. Walsh had been around this town ever since he was a small lad. 'You've grown into a strapping lad, Ryan — how come you're not married yet?'

'I haven't found the right lady.' Why was it that if you were a little shy and over thirty, people expected you to be married and have children?

'There will be someone out there for you,' Mrs. Walsh said.

She had a twinkle in her eye as she passed him his cup of coffee. Her head slightly tilted towards Melissa. Ryan looked over. There would be no way that he would be interested in someone like her. She seemed to him to be one of those high-maintenance girls, who for-ever wanted the latest designer clothes and expensive foreign holidays. Suzie, on the other hand, seemed such a genuine person: someone he would be happy to come home to at night. *Ryan, what are you saying?* He tried to get any thoughts of dating out of his head. Sharon had been enough for a lifetime. Jamie over at the pub always tried flirting with him, but she didn't interest him either.

Taking his cup, he passed a few tables full of people typing madly away on laptops, or with pen and paper in hand. Melissa was sat nursing a cup of tea, whilst a small silver teapot stood on the table. Ryan took his seat by the window, pretending to people-watch — not that there were many people walking around at this time.

Rooting in his jacket pocket, he pulled out his mobile phone, setting it on video mode, then left it on the chair next to him, hoping that if Melissa said anything he would be able to capture it. The café had started to empty. Melissa, along with a host of other people, walked out of the door. Mrs. Walsh came around the counter, a cloth and spray in her hands, and proceeded to wipe the tables.

Ryan couldn't see anything else he could do. 'Great coffee as always, Mrs. Walsh.'

'You off too? Aye, suppose you will be off into Weymouth to one of those nightclubs.'

'Not tonight. I have a bit too much to do at home,' Ryan replied, giving her a smile.

Ryan left, quickly looking up and down both sides of the street to see where Melissa had gone. Damn it, she'd disappeared. He cancelled the video recording and checked his phone. An envelope flashed on his screen, indicating a message. He wasn't sure if it was just his father again, with his incessant complaining about the golf course. How slow the planning committee was being — way too slow! — how the population of Castle Cove was against the plan. Ryan had had enough of it, but he didn't want to end up with no money, not until he had enough cash to be able to support himself.

Yes, he worked for his father and got a very basic wage, which was not enough to live on independently. But all his father's luxury comforts were his to enjoy. *Why does life have to be so hard to navigate at times?* Ryan gave himself a mental shake: he was meant to be looking at his messages, not worrying about things he couldn't control.

The message was from Suzie, to say that she had found a clue, and would he go over to the pub? Quickly, he tapped out a text back to say he had lost Melissa, and would be over in a few minutes.

Ryan set off down Old Castle Road towards the pub. Just as he walked around the bend he spotted Melissa, who had what he presumed was a phone against her ear, although he couldn't hear what she was saying from where he was currently standing. There were no cars or people around at this time, so Ryan walked as quietly as he could.

'I've got a new murder mystery story. I wrote it in longhand. Once I have typed it up then I will email it over. I'm sure you're going to love it.'

Ryan didn't think much of the conversation Melissa was having — who cared if she had written another story? Picking up his pace, he jogged over to the Castle Arms, throwing open the door. His eyes searched for Suzie from the doorway. Jamie was behind the bar tonight, now sporting a pink mohican. She hadn't changed one bit since she was a kid — she'd always been one to be different.

Des was wiping down empty tables, while Suzie was collecting glasses over near the pool tables at the back of the pub. Ryan made a beeline for her, parking himself against a pool table. He looked around to make sure that they couldn't be overheard.

'We need to talk, Ryan,' she said.

'I saw Melissa in the café, and then again on Old Castle Road.'

'What was she doing?'

'She was on the phone, blabbing about some new crime manuscript she had written.'

Suzie's face fell and her eyes flashed with anger. 'That isn't her manuscript — she stole it off Crystal! I went over to the hotel and asked Colin if he could let me into her room. It was in there.'

'How do you know it was Crystal's manuscript?'

'I marked the manuscript in red, suggesting changes, on the backs of the first few chapters. It was sat on the dressing table with my corrections all over it.'

Ryan didn't fully understand why he was doing all this legwork, but Suzie intrigued him, and he would love to get to know her better. He wanted her to stay in Castle Cove, but he knew that in a few days she would probably be going back to London. How could he get her to stay?

'That doesn't mean anything, unless you know for certain that Melissa stole it.' Ryan couldn't understand what was going on. 'Why are you so bothered?'

'Because if I can prove she stole one manuscript, I can prove that she stole two. I know you don't get it, but please trust me.'

'I do, Suzie, even after so short an acquaintance, and I don't do that often. It takes me a while to trust anyone.'

'Thanks — I think.' Suzie folded her arms over her chest. 'Crystal seemed like a really sweet person. She didn't deserve to die, and I want the person who killed her to pay. I don't think Melissa killed her, for all she is a bitch. I very much doubt that she has it in her.' She sighed. 'Crystal left the Castle Arms at about ten . . . '

'Why are you running around trying to get to the bottom of things?'

'Did you know I was arrested for Crystal's murder?'

'You said.'

Suzie saw the bored look etched onto Ryan's face. 'Look, regardless of what you think, I have already been accused of doing something I didn't, and was unable to clear my name. This time, I am determined to prove my innocence.'

He held his hands up. 'Okay, okay. I will help. So, what do we do now?'

'That, I don't know. I'm crawling around in the dark.'

'We will figure it out.'

'Look, Ryan, can you hang around? I need to get all these glasses into the dishwasher.'

She had already left Des in the lurch

today without so much as a by-your-leave. She wandered over to the farthest table, collecting all the glasses, and then began stacking the dishwasher. If she was going to get a job, she needed to keep Des sweet, so hopefully he would decide that he wanted another permanent barmaid.

15

Suzie collected the last of the glasses, locked the pub and made sure all the tables were clean and tidy. Ryan waited patiently, sitting on a pool table. He was a sweetheart.

'You can get off now lass, thanks for helping out. Are you sure that you have to go back to London? There's a job here if you want it.' Des said winking at her.

She was considering staying. The little cottage looked so sweet, and she supposed that it would be within her price range. Her flat in London should be worth more than the cottage. Suzie decided that she would message them and put an offer in on the house. She liked it here, even though she still had DI Tay thinking badly of her.

'Ryan, we need to go to the police station and speak to DI Tay.'

'Why?'

'Look, we found the laptop and we

need them to check it. We even found the manuscript in Melissa's room. Without them looking at the evidence, then they won't believe me. Bill says they are just dying to re-arrest me and charge me with murder.'

Suzie looked imploringly at Ryan. If he didn't believe her, then who would?

'Okay, come on. Though I'm not sure that he will be on duty now . . . '

Ryan couldn't believe he was being dragged around town on a wild-goose chase. The thing that got him more was that he liked spending time in Suzie's company. She was someone he could fall in love with. Oh, who was he kidding? He had fallen for her the first time he had seen her in the middle of the road.

Even though he could understand why she wanted to clear her name, he still thought she should leave it to the professionals. Honestly, he was sure Suzie was going to be the death of him!

'Come on, we'll walk. It will do us both good to get some fresh air for a change.'

Suzie laughed heartily. 'Isn't that what we have been doing? I think we've been outside together more than we've been in.'

'That's true; I think I'm going dizzy with all this running around in circles.' Ryan gave her a gentle shove.

'I'm walking, I'm walking, Mr. Bossy Boots.'

'So, what do you think happened?'

'I think that the death of Crystal is to do with the manuscript. I did initially think that it was to do with the golf course. Yet I couldn't see the writer of those notes becoming a murderer. Whoever wrote those notes was just trying to threaten someone: I doubt they would resort to killing.'

'So whoever it is would be desperate?'

'Yes, they would be — but why? Why would anyone be that desperate to steal someone's work?' A thought hit Suzie: perhaps she should put out feelers and see how Melissa's books were doing. If she was making money on the sales of her titles, there was a site Suzie could use called Book Check which would give her a rough idea of Melissa's success. Suzie wasn't sure why she hadn't thought of it before.

'Ryan, do you have any data available on your phone?'

'Yes, why?'

'Well, I want to check out a novel, and see how many copies it has shifted,' Suzie said, holding out her hand.

Ryan took his phone out of his jacket pocket and handed it to her.

'Thank you.' Suzie typed in the website address, and then checked Melissa Spencer's name. 'Looks like Melissa's books aren't selling well. Even after all the publicity that one got through the court case,' she added absentmindedly.

'What?'

'Look . . . that graph there shows the approximate sales of a book. The other shows where the book is in the sales charts on particular websites.'

'Oh, I see.'

But Susie didn't think he did see. Ryan wasn't an author; he didn't know that seeing your book disappear into nothingness once it was printed was one of the hardest things to deal with. That, or the wait for an answer from a publisher.

A cold wind blew down her neck, making her shiver. Suzie shuddered; it was like someone was walking over her grave.

She was glad when she reached the police station. It looked smaller from this side. When she had been arrested, she had been taken through the car park and through the security door.

A policewoman was on the reception desk. 'Can I help you?'

'We'd like to speak to DI Tay, please. My name is Ryan Arnley.'

'I will just see if he is still here — he may have gone home by now. Take a seat over there and I will see if I can locate him.'

Suzie and Ryan sat down on the hard blue plastic chairs against the wall. They sat in complete silence as they waited. Suzie, hoping that the detective inspector would be around, was trying to formulate in her mind what she was going to say. After what seemed like hours, Detective Bill walked through the door on their left.

'Suzie, is everything alright?'

'We wanted to see DI Tay, but I think

you will do,' she said, smiling.

'DI Tay has taken a few days' leave. I think the top brass are trying to put him out to pasture. So, how can I help?'

Suzie took out her phone. 'Look at these pictures.' She showed him the photographs she had taken at the hotel. 'I need you to do a search of the hotel and to check Melissa Spencer's room. But you also need to make it look like you are removing things from a few other rooms, too.'

'Why? I have to justify this to my superiors. I trust you, but you have to give me something.'

'The manuscript.'

'What about it? Suzie, look . . . I know you want to help, but you're really not giving me anything to work with here.'

'I found the manuscript that I had written on. It's in Melissa Spencer's room, and I am sure my laptop is too. When I first got the laptop, I marked the base of it with one of those security pens. I'm sure if you take a UV light to it, then you will see what I have written on the back. Then, when you have checked, I will tell you what I wrote.'

'Okay — supposing you are right, how do your propose to help? I have an idea . . . but it would only work if you and DI Tay helped, too.'

Suzie explained her plan to the policeman. When she had finished, a huge smile appeared on Bill's face. 'Are you sure that you are an author and not a detective?'

'I'm sure. I don't think I have the stomach for that.'

The three of them talked for a while longer, until they had reached a full agreement on the plan.

'If you take the laptop, can I borrow it for the murder mystery night?'

'Yes, I guess so. And if it is proved to be yours, then — ' He paused. 'Well, we will need to keep it for evidence, but I will make a point in the press conference that it is yours. Would that help?'

Suzie couldn't believe what he had just said. 'Yes, it would be a big help.'

Ryan squeezed her hand for comfort. Maybe she would be able to clear her name after all?

After about an hour at the police station, the two of them left Bill. He would still need to organise whatever he intended to do, but at least he was doing something.

'What do you think, Ryan? Do you think that I am totally crazy?'

'No, I don't. Be careful, Suzie. I wouldn't want anything to happen to you.'

'Ryan, I will be careful.'

Ryan brought her into his arms and just held her. Suzie felt like she was in heaven. Could this be real?

16

Laurie sat behind the desk of the library. Her leg was still sore from her near miss with the car, and the last thing that she needed was to have Suzie Cail in the library.

She could see that Suzie didn't know whether to sit down or stand. Laurie had made it clear that she hadn't been one of her favourite people here in Castle Cove, being very plain about the fact that she didn't want her around.

'Laurie, I know we haven't always got on, but I wondered if you would listen to me.'

'Are you going to try and run me down again?'

'What are you talking about?' Suzie asked, gobsmacked.

'Someone tried to run me over. You drove the car straight at me! If I hadn't fallen out of the way, I doubt I would be here today,' Laurie replied.

'You're serious, aren't you? Why would anyone try and hurt you?'

'How am I meant to know? Ask yourself why you did it!'

Suzie couldn't believe what she was hearing. Laurie seriously thought that she would stoop so low as to try and hurt someone! She really did have her wrong. 'I haven't even used my car all the time I have been here.'

'What colour car was it?' Ryan asked.

'It was a black one.'

'That proves it wasn't me,' Suzie declared. 'My car is red. Please listen to me, and then maybe — just maybe — you will change your mind. If you're worried about the car, I can give you my number plate and you can check that MOT thingy. It tells you on there what colour the car is.'

Laurie looked thoughtful. The silence was deafening. Finally, she spoke. 'Go on, then. You have five minutes, and I suggest you don't hang around. I have a murder mystery event to oversee, and the last thing I need is for the festival to be a flop on the final night.' She took a slow and deliberate sip of her coffee. 'Okay — first things first . . . '

Susie waited, wondering what Laurie could possibly mean.

'Why should I believe anything you say? I didn't want someone like you at my festival. You got yourself arrested for murder. Tell me why I should trust you?'

'This is,' she said, holding up a red laptop, 'Melissa's — well, supposedly. The thing is, I once had a red laptop too. On the bottom, in security pen, I drew a flower and wrote my postcode.' Suzie put the laptop upside down on the desk. Reaching into her pocket, she pulled out her purse. Taking out her driving licence, she placed it in front of Laurie.

'Here — use this, and scan the bottom of the laptop.' Ryan handed Laurie a UV torch.

'Laurie,' Suzie said, 'do it so I can't see. Then, once you have looked, it will either confirm to you whether I have lied — or have been telling the truth all along.'

Suzie could see the look of contempt on Laurie's face. It was obvious she still didn't believe her. But Laurie did as she had been asked. Taking the torch, she shone it on the computer, slowly going over the base. In the middle suddenly appeared a flower — badly drawn, but nonetheless a flower. Off to the right-hand side was a postcode. Laurie held the UV light over the number whilst she scanned the driving license.

'The postcodes match,' she said in utter disbelief.

'As I said, it's my laptop. This is the computer Melissa said was hers. She also had Crystal's manuscript in her room — the one I had looked at, and made a couple of changes to in red pen. The one the police found showed no red pen on any of the pages.'

'But . . . '

'But, nothing. So, now I have proved my innocence — at least to you — are you going to help me?'

Laurie nodded slowly. 'What do you need me to do?'

Suzie looked at Ryan, and then back at Laurie. 'This murder mystery night tonight . . . I need you to change it. To make it about the murder that happened here in Castle Cove. I'm going to see if DI Tay and Bill will come. We can unmask the killer if all goes well.'

The silence which descended upon the room was deafening. Suzie hoped that the papers would pick this up, and she would clear her name. Everyone in the country would see that she had been innocent all the time. Her publisher would be happy to take her books. Or maybe she should find herself a new agent and publisher — people who would believe her.

'Okay, well, you need to tell me what you need me to do,' Laurie said. 'I owe you an apology for everything. And I'd love it if you came back next year, and gave a talk at the festival.'

Susie smiled.

After telling Laurie the plan, she and Ryan left the library, a spring in their step. Bill had already seen the photos that she had taken of Melissa's room, with the laptop in situ. They would hurry to replace it — hopefully Colin would be able to get Melissa out of the room for a while, so they could complete the mission. Susie needed to phone Bill and ask him to check out the room with crime scene investigators whilst they were at the Castle Arms. This would come off — at least, she hoped so.

'Everything is set, Ryan.' Her voice was shaky.

Ryan turned to face her, brushing a loose tendril of hair off her face. 'Suzie, honey. Everything will work out, I promise. You sorted my father out, didn't you?'

'That wasn't hard to do. I mean, using your own paper for threatening notes! It only occurred to me when I sat and thought about how the hotel was in the way.'

Ryan moved closer. Suzie didn't move away, just stayed exactly where she was, inviting him into her space. Leaning forward, he wrapped his arms around her, bringing Suzie into his embrace and kissing her gently. Then he deepened the kiss, and everything around her went hazy as for that moment there were only the two of them in the world.

Suzie was the one who broke the magic first. 'Come on, we need to get moving.

As much as I would love to stay here with you, we're not going to get anywhere until we get over to the pub.'

Ryan nodded his assent. Suzie took his hand, and together they walked back to the Castle Arms. It had become her base whilst she had been here. She liked coming back to the pub — Castle Cove felt like home now. Suzie hoped that her offer on the cottage would be accepted. Then the new friends she had made, who she was loath to leave, would become permanent.

Ryan held the pub door open for her; she walked past him and squeezed his arm. Des was already putting the tables into rows, leaving only the pool tables to be moved. The actors would need a largish space for their performance — hopefully it will be show-stopping. Suzie smiled to herself; they needed to get moving. 'Ryan, could you help Des move the pool tables, please?'

'Sure thing.'

Ryan left her side. She could see him and Des chatting and laughing. It was nice to see Ryan smiling; especially now things seemed to have settled down for him at home.

Suzie thought she had better get changed. She walked past the phone, which reminded her she needed to contact Meg — perhaps she would come over for a bit of entertainment. Taking her mobile out of her pocket, she called her friend. 'Hi, Meg. It's Susie. Do you want to come to the pub tonight? I've been told there will be some fireworks. Yes, I thought you would like to watch the show.'

'Great — see you later!'

Susie put her phone away. She started walking up the stairs — her feet stuck to the carpet. Pulling them up hard, she made a mental note to hire a carpet cleaner and give the pub a good going-over. As long as she would still have a job here, it was surprising how much she was enjoying the freedom of not having to write, and just living life without being chained to a word processor.

Suzie jumped in the shower, letting the cool water wash over her. Her stomach was doing somersaults: she was scared. There was a murderer about, and she and her crew of sleuths had set a trap. It could be dangerous for them all . . . but if it worked, life in Castle Cove could continue as before, and Crystal would get justice.

Suzie dried herself quickly, dressing from head to foot in black, her beige handbag the only splash of colour. She sent a message to DI Tay and Bill to see if they were ready for the night's events. Then she phoned the estate agent and put an offer in for the cottage. He said it needed some modernisation, and a viewing would be beneficial but not entirely necessary. Suzie said it would be all right — she was pretty handy at DIY, and if it needed a major overhaul then she would phone around and get tradesmen in to do the work.

She sat on the bed, trawling through the internet for estate agents in London. She left several voicemail messages for different ones, asking them to come and view her flat and see about getting it sold.

Back downstairs, the pub was filling

up with people. Little place cards told people where to sit. Melissa would be sat with Bill, whilst DI Tay would be with Suzie and Ryan. Hopefully, Laurie had debriefed the actors; she had told Suzie that they usually ad-libbed the speech. All they had was a plot and the clues, then they just said what they thought sounded best.

Suzie couldn't ask for anything better. But she was still nervous; hopefully, by the end of it all she would be able to relax. *If this goes wrong, it doesn't bear thinking about — Suzie, stop worrying!*

Laurie arrived, wearing a bright green skirt and matching top, clutching her clipboard. It made Suzie smile. She dressed similarly to Jamie's strange and unusual style, which worked for them.

Laurie pushed through the crowds, making a beeline for the bar. 'Suzie, can I have a quick word please?'

'Sure, Laurie, come through.' Suzie nodded towards the staff-only door.

As she guided Laurie first, for some reason she had a feeling they were being watched. Suzie felt the hairs on the back of her neck stand on end. She turned slowly. Melissa, in all her finery, was watching their every move.

'Laurie, we are being watched. I wouldn't be surprised if we were being listened to as well.'

Laurie nodded. 'I just wanted to check what entrances the actors should use, and where they can get changed.'

'Oh, Des is so silly not to have told you already. They can come through the kitchen if they like, or through the main door. Are there any props you need that you don't have?'

A shadow moved past the other side of the door. Someone was listening — they needed to watch what they were saying. Suzie tried to indicate this to Laurie, but she merely nodded; obviously she had seen the shadow cast herself.

'Can I use both? The pub door as the front door; and the kitchen for, say, another part of the house?'

'Of course you can and I am really looking forward to it. I hope I am allowed to guess the killer?'

The two of them laughed. Suzie found

it amazing: after everything that had happened between them, these were the first nice words they had said to each other.

Laurie led them out, and with a quick nod of the head she was gone. Suzie took her place behind the bar. Most people had already taken their seats, drinks in hand, as the starters were being brought out from the kitchen.

Several people had dressed up in 1950s outfits, as the theme was 'A 1950s Wedding Murder'. Suzie did wonder exactly what Laurie had changed it to now. It had been hard to gain her trust. Hopefully she had, or else tonight would be a real flop. With all the journalists here, the story should be on the front pages of all the local papers — and maybe some national ones, too.

Melissa had arrived on the arm of Colin. She was dressed in a red puff skirt — adorned with a little black dog silhouette — and a white top, looking like she had just stepped out of the film *Grease*.

Suzie took her seat. Ryan hadn't turned

up yet; she wasn't even sure he would come. She was filled with disappointment — she had obviously misunderstood his intentions. Ryan was the sort of guy she could easily have fallen in love with.

Just as she was lamenting her lot in life, Ryan walked towards her with Meg on his arm.

'I thought I would pick Meg up, seeing as Colin seems to have his hands full,' Ryan said by way of an apology.

'I thought . . . '

'You thought I was going to stand you up?'

Suzie hung her head. 'Yes. Something like that.'

Laurie stood up, ready to address the crowd. The room fell silent.

'Good evening, ladies and gents. We have a change to the scheduled Murder Mystery, but I hope it won't be too disappointing.' She looked quickly at her notes. 'Tonight we will be trying to solve 'The Sunny Day Killing'. Once everyone has received their starters, we will begin. Remember to look for the clues; and, as always, the boards will hold extra pieces of information given throughout the evening. Tonight we have a few special actors: DI Tay and Bill will be acting as the detectives. Even our beloved landlord will be taking a small role. Not everyone will give you correct information — it is your job to discover the fact from the fiction.'

Several guests applauded. Meg patted Suzie's hand. 'You know, I am really looking forward to this.'

'Me too.' She nodded her agreement.

One of the actresses started speaking. 'How dare you think my novel is rubbish? You are the one that should give up — you can't write!'

'Fine, that's your opinion — but I will only take that sort of criticism from an editor. The day *they* tell me that I can't write is the day I give up,' said another.

The play went on for a while longer in the same vein, until the part where the evidence was shown. The laptop was used as a vital example. Suzie looked over at Melissa, who was shuffling in her seat. This made her smile. DI Tay and Bill played their parts with aplomb.

When the show ended an hour and a half later, one of the actors dressed in a waiter's outfit collected everybody's evidence sheets and took them with him into the back of the pub. Time slowed down. Suzie kept checking her watch and seeing how long it had been.

Bill winked in her direction as the guy in a tux came back with the sheets in his hand. Then he got up and took centre stage.

'As you have all seen, this murder has been one of those screwy cases, where the death of a young author took place on a summer evening.' Bill looked down at his police notebook, then called each of the actors in turn to stand up.

'Miss Ashford, you wanted the Queen of Crime award. I believe you would have done anything to get up there on top — all except murder.'

A few groans went around, obviously from the people who had chosen Miss Ashford.

'Mr. Arnley, you wanted to ruin the town, but I doubt that you are capable of murder either. Even if I disagree with your business decisions.'

Bill continued to go around several people, asking them to stand up, which made Suzie uncomfortable because everyone stared at you.

'Suzie Cail, please stand. You were accused of the murder originally, as well as of theft. The evidence which has been provided has cleared you of every wrongdoing.'

Mr. Waiter then stood in front. 'Unfortunately, no one has chosen the correct murderer. I will leave it to Bill. He will, in his own special way, let you all in on who killed the author and why.'

Several bulbs flashed from the cameramen that were there. Journalists moved further to the front so they could hear over the noise of the room.

Bill took a step forward. Everyone was transfixed at the goings-on in front of them. Suzie was the only one who realised that DI Tay was now standing guard at the pub door. Des stood in front of the kitchen entrance as if interested in the night's entertainment.

'You see, the crime wasn't just

committed this week. But perhaps I am not the best person to tell you the story. Suzie, can you come up here, please?'

Suzie got slowly out of her seat and walked to the front, feeling many pairs of eyes watching her every move. She cleared her throat before she spoke.

'It started when a piece of evidence that has been presented tonight — the laptop — was stolen. It contained a manuscript, which was then used to produce a book. The original author of that manuscript was slated in the media and by the court.'

Suzie watched Bill as he purposefully looked around the whole room. She presumed that he was making sure they were taking in what she was saying. Especially the journalists — and the killer.

'Next came a literary festival, its aim being to keep the library open. Instead of fun and frolics, there was murder. The laptop, which had been stolen a year before has been officially proven to belong to an innocent victim. What we couldn't have known is that if we had followed yet another stolen manuscript, then this murder would have been solved the day it happened. You see, when I came here, I wanted nothing more than to forget I was Suzie Cail.'

She looked at Ryan and Meg, who gave her reassuring smiles. 'A debut author spoke to me on Friday, asking me if I would read her new crime novel. I agreed, and marked the changes in red pen. Yet when her dead body was discovered, the manuscript was missing. Several people around here had been told she was a new author, and how she had written a crime novel. It looked as if people were interested.'

'I don't have to listen to this.' Melissa stood up and turned to walk away.

Two undercover police officers stood at either side of her table, shaking their heads. Melissa sulkily sat back down.

Suzie continued. 'I hated that all the fingers pointed at me.'

Someone in the audience shouted, 'Hurry up — get to the point!'

'I am. You see, the author that stole my work — and also Crystal's — is here.

Melissa Spencer, who killed Crystal with a blow to the head. We can only surmise what happened immediately before that. Crystal could have realised that her manuscript had been stolen. Or she received a call to go and meet someone with her work. Either way, at midnight she left the hotel with an envelope of some kind. CCTV tells us that much. If she saw who had stolen her manuscript, or lured her out, then that person would want rid of her. They wanted to make sure that she couldn't tell anyone.'

Suzie took a sip of her drink and looked at all the people in the crowd. They looked shell-shocked; this wasn't the night that they had expected.

'It's my belief that Crystal saw who had stolen her precious book — her baby — and confronted them on the beach. This was a strange case. I was arrested under the belief that I was guilty. But actually Crystal had become my friend, and I wanted to discover who had killed her. So I set out to find out who the killer was. The trail pointing to them is clear. Although I am not a police officer, and only an ex-author, I will leave the rest of the evidence to the police.' Suzie walked back to her seat.

Everyone was aghast. Melissa stood up once again. 'Trying to make everyone feel sorry for you? Suzie, I thought you'd sunk so low when you stole my manuscript — and here you are now, pointing the finger at an innocent party.'

'No, Melissa. I know who killed Crystal. I admit, I thought that the missing manuscript was a red herring, and that her ex-boyfriend Mathew had killed her for the advance she had received. But I was wrong — the manuscript had everything to do with it.' Suzie stared icily at Melissa.

'Oh, I've heard enough. I thought that this was going to be a fun night out, not a set-up.'

'I admit we changed the mystery, because we knew what had happened and it was easier to confront the killer.'

'Melissa Spencer,' said one of the undercover policemen, taking hold of her arm, 'you are under arrest for the murder of Crystal Siena.'

'I didn't do anything!' Melissa protested, and tried to struggle free.

Just for a moment, Suzie felt sorry for her . . . but then the thought disappeared. She knew she had done the right thing.

Melissa was placed in handcuffs and led away. The room lit up like a Belisha beacon with all the flashbulbs from the cameras. Suzie wanted to shout with joy, but now was not the time. Besides, her heart was pounding.

Ryan gave her a peck on the cheek. 'I promise you a better one later.'

'Suzie, you solved the murder. I've not had so much fun in my life before.' Meg picked up her drink and took a small sip before continuing. 'I wish you were staying here.'

'Well, it's a good job I have put in an offer for the cottage on your row, then. I have to sell my flat in London. I had thought about just getting all my things and bringing them here, but I wasn't sure about storage facilities.'

Ryan piped up, 'You can leave them at the pub, or at mine.'

Des added, 'Let's go down to London

tomorrow with a van, and just pack everything up?'

Suzie liked that idea, and she didn't think that Jess would care she was moving. Since the court case she had been distant anyway. Here in Castle Cove she felt at home, that she was wanted. Standing here with Ryan's arms around her and her new friends was just the best feeling ever.

'Why don't we just go and get everything tonight?' Des asked, a serious look on his face, just like a schoolteacher did when they were telling you off. Everyone laughed.

Tomorrow, when the papers came out, Suzie's name would be in the clear. Perhaps she might even use this murder in a book. It was going to be quite the adventure, moving to a small seaside town, and having a gorgeous boyfriend and job waiting there for her. Suzie had never felt so lucky.

We do hope that you have enjoyed reading this large print book.

Did you know that all of our titles are available for purchase?

We publish a wide range of high quality large print books including:

Romances, Mysteries, Classics
General Fiction
Non Fiction and Westerns

Special interest titles available in large print are:

The Little Oxford Dictionary
Music Book, Song Book
Hymn Book, Service Book

Also available from us courtesy of Oxford University Press:

Young Readers' Dictionary
(large print edition)
Young Readers' Thesaurus
(large print edition)

For further information or a free brochure, please contact us at:
Ulverscroft Large Print Books Ltd.,
The Green, Bradgate Road, Anstey,
Leicester, LE7 7FU, England.
Tel: (00 44) **0116 236 4325**
Fax: (00 44) **0116 234 0205**

ADVANCE SOUTH!

John Robb

An expedition is digging at Lukka Oasis in search of a lost civilisation. But when valuable gold coins are uncovered, the men are massacred by their Arab bearers, and only a woman escapes. When a party of three legionnaires decides to desert from Post D, each has his own good reason for doing so. Their first destination: Lukka Oasis. But in escaping from the Legion post, they inadvertently set fire to it. What follows is a fight for survival in the desert, with danger and death stalking all parties involved . . .